A *pickup truck came out of the darkness,*

but Lisa's first impression of the driver was far from reassuring.

He was powerfully built, with broad shoulders and a chest to match. He had a roughly chiseled face, with dark, slashing brows. Unshaven, with a thick mane of black hair, he looked tough and dangerous.

Exactly the kind of man she didn't want to meet alone on a highway at night.

He came toward her, and his gaze went over her boldly, from her short auburn hair down the length of her body. Lisa's breath caught. Fear tightened her stomach.

Refusing to give in to it, she lifted her head and met his eyes defiantly. "I don't need any help."

He smiled slightly. "That so?" His voice was like velvet rubbed over gravel. He looked from her to her disabled car and back again. "You could have fooled me."

Dear Reader,

Spring is on its way in at last, but we've got some hot books to keep you warm during the last few chilly days. There's our American Hero title, for example: Ann Williams's *Cold, Cold Heart.* Here's a man who has buried all his feelings, all his hopes and dreams, a man whose job it is to rescue missing children—and who can't get over the tragedy of failure. Into his life comes a woman he can't resist, a woman whose child has been stolen from her, and suddenly he's putting it all on the line all over again. He's back to saving children—and back to dreaming of love. Will his cold heart melt? You take a guess!

Mary Anne Wilson completes her "Sister, Sister" duet with *Two Against the World.* For all of you who loved *Two for the Road,* here's the sequel you've been waiting for. And if you missed the first book, don't worry. You can still order a copy—just don't let Ali's story slip through your hands in the meantime!

The rest of the month is filled with both familiar names—like Maura Seger and Amanda Stevens—and new ones—like Diana Whitney, who makes her Intimate Moments debut, and Dani Criss, who's publishing her very first book. I think you'll enjoy everything we have to offer, as well as everything that will be heading your way in months to come. And speaking of the future, look for some real excitement next month, when Intimate Moments celebrates its tenth anniversary with a can't-miss lineup of books, including Patricia Gardner Evans's long-awaited American Hero title, *Quinn Eisley's War.* Come May, Intimate Moments is definitely *the* place to be.

Yours,
Leslie J. Wainger
Senior Editor and Editorial Coordinator

MAN

OF THE

HOUR

Maura
Seger

Silhouette® INTIMATE MOMENTS®

Published by Silhouette Books New York

America's Publisher of Contemporary Romance

SILHOUETTE BOOKS
300 East 42nd St., New York, N.Y. 10017

MAN OF THE HOUR

ISBN: 0-373-07492-1

First Silhouette Books printing April 1993

Printed in the U.S.A.

MAURA SEGER

and her husband, Michael, met while they were both working for the same company. Married after a whirlwind courtship that might have been taken directly from a romance novel, Maura credits her husband's patient support and good humor with helping her fulfill the lifelong dream of being a writer.

Currently writing contemporaries for Silhouette Books and historicals for Harlequin Books and mainstream, she finds that writing each book is an adventure filled with fascinating people who never fail to surprise her.

Prologue

With every mile that vanished down the long white line of the highway, Lisa felt safer. With every hour that passed through the long rain-splattered night, she relaxed a little more. With every soft sound and muffled movement from the back seat, she strengthened in her resolve.

Jimmy slept under the old Hudson Bay blanket, clutching his battered Bunky Bear, oblivious to the world. He slept just as he had in his bed in the New York apartment, fair hair tousled, thick lashes shadowing freckled cheeks, lips slightly parted, lost in a four-year-old's dreams.

For his mother there was no rest. Nor would there be until she was convinced they were truly beyond the cold, frightening danger that had crept into her very soul.

She had been driving since early afternoon and it was now only a few hours until dawn. Her eyes were dry, her head throbbed and the ache in the small of her back was incessant.

None of that mattered. She had a single goal that had kept her going throughout the seemingly endless night. When she finally caught the first glimpse of it, she let out a long sigh of relief.

Langston, the sign on the side of the road read, 3 Miles.

Almost there, she thought, and pressed down a little harder on the accelerator. Perhaps because she was so very tired and more than a bit distracted, she wasn't paying as close attention as she should have been.

But it was also dark. She might not have seen the small piece of wood studded with nails lying in the center of the road under any circumstances.

The car struck the wood without warning. Immediately, it began to lose speed.

Lisa cried out and fought to keep the vehicle straight, but the steering was suddenly heavy and sluggish. It was all she could do to maneuver over to the side of the road and coast to a stop.

She sat for a moment, her hands still gripping the wheel and her heart pounding, as she tried to think of what could have happened. Much as she hated to admit it, cars were a mystery to her. She knew where to put the gas and could check her own oil, but beyond that she didn't have a clue.

Her stiff legs protested as she straightened them and got out. The night air was cool and damp. Jimmy continued to sleep peacefully.

Reassured that at least he was all right, she stared at the car. Her first thought, that maybe she had a flat, was quickly proved wrong. All the tires were fine. Baffled, she lifted the hood and peered under it.

The tangle of wires, hoses and metal told her nothing. Obviously there was a problem, but she couldn't begin to figure out what it was, much less solve it.

Which meant that she was stuck, still several miles from her destination, on the highway at night, with an exhausted four-year-old and no idea of what to do next.

The last service station she'd seen was a good ten miles down the road in the opposite direction. There were several closer by in Langston, but she doubted they'd be open at this hour. If she'd had a car phone, she could have called for help, but she'd hesitated to spend the money on one.

She took a deep breath and told herself not to panic. Things could have been a lot worse. The moment when she'd felt as though she were losing control of the car replayed in her mind.

If anyone else had been nearby, there could have been a serious accident. Jimmy could have been hurt. Instead he was fine. That was all that really mattered.

Even so, her throat tightened. She was so damn tired and she'd been under so much stress for so long. Just when she'd begun to think she'd made it, this had to happen. The darkness pressed in around her.

She shut her eyes against the tears that threatened to fall. There was no way she would cry. She was a grown woman with a child to care for. She had to get a grip on herself, sort things out, decide what to—

The sound of an engine broke the silence. Relief poured through her. Lisa took a step closer to the road only to stop abruptly. A pickup truck came out of the darkness. The glare of its headlights made her flinch.

She put a hand up to protect her eyes but lowered it quickly as the vehicle neared to see who was behind the wheel. Her first impression was far from reassuring.

The driver was young, not more than a few years older than herself, and powerfully built, with broad shoulders and a chest to match. He had a lean face, roughly chiseled, with dark, slashing brows, high cheekbones and a square jaw. Unshaven, with a thick mane of black hair, he looked tough and dangerous.

Exactly the kind of man she didn't want to meet alone on a highway at night.

For a moment she allowed herself to believe that he would keep going but the truck inexorably slowed and came to a stop not far beyond her own car. The man got out, rising to a full height that was several inches over six feet, and came toward her.

Lisa's breath caught. He was even bigger and more powerfully muscled than she'd thought. Dressed in an old plaid shirt that was open at the collar and wearing well-worn jeans, he looked as though he'd stepped from another age, one where men lived by their own rules and on their own terms.

The look he gave her suggested he agreed with her summation. His gaze went over her boldly, from the top of her short, feathery auburn hair, down the length of her slender body clad in a mauve cotton pullover she'd pulled on hastily without stopping to think that it had shrunk in the wash, to the forest green silk pants that hugged her derriere.

Against her will, Lisa blushed. She couldn't remember the last time a man's scrutiny had made her so vividly aware of herself as a woman. Fear tightened her stomach. Refusing to give in to it, she lifted her head and met his eyes defiantly.

"I don't need any help."

He stopped, put his hands on his narrow hips, and smiled slightly. "That so?"

His voice was deep but pleasant. It sounded like velvet rubbed over gravel. He looked from her to the car and back again. "You could have fooled me. What's the trouble?"

Lisa hesitated. Now that he was actually talking to her, he didn't seem quite so threatening. In fact, there was something about him...she couldn't put her finger on it, but it was oddly reassuring. Big he was, and undeniably tough, yet the more she studied him, the more she thought...

Her eyes widened. He couldn't be...could he?

"Mark?" she murmured. "Mark Fletcher?"

He nodded curtly and for a moment he seemed almost displeased at having been recognized. But that fled as he took another long hard look at her. He took a step closer as if to confirm what his eyes were telling him.

"Lisa Morley?"

She nodded. A small laugh escaped her. "You scared the daylights out of me."

He frowned, honestly puzzled. "How come?"

She started to explain, realized she couldn't and shrugged. "It's been a long time."

His smile returned but this time it reached all the way to his startlingly light blue eyes. "Ten years. What happened to all the hair you used to have?"

Her self-consciousness returned. She was amazed that he'd remember such a thing. She'd had long hair all through high school. Mark had been two years ahead of her, but they'd known each other all the same, sort of.

He was the bad boy from the wrong side of town with a penchant for fast cars, cold beer and girls who wore spandex.

She wasn't precisely Miss Goody Two-shoes, but she'd grown up protected and loved, and she'd aimed to stay that way. Except for an occasional long, simmering glance across the cafeteria, they'd kept their distance.

Until now.

"I cut it," she said. "It was too much trouble to take care of."

He studied her a moment longer. "Looks nice this way, too. Now suppose you tell me what you're doing here on the side of the road in the middle of the night."

"I ran over something, a piece of wood, I think. The car started losing power and I had trouble controlling it."

He walked past her to take a look under the hood. Lisa took a deep, restoring breath. She couldn't deny now that she was glad to see him.

The fear she'd felt seemed foolish yet it wasn't completely gone. Whatever else he was or had been, safe wasn't a word anyone associated with Mark Fletcher.

She watched, trying not to stare at the long muscular line of his back as he bent over the engine. The plaid shirt stretched tautly over his broad shoulders. The jeans he wore were looser, they looked chosen purely for comfort, but they couldn't conceal the undeniably attractive tautness of his bottom or the long sinewy legs that moved with such easy grace.

He straightened, brushed off his hands and turned back to her. "Busted fan belt. Whatever you hit must have gone right through it. Any chance you've got a spare?"

Glumly, she shook her head. A spare tire she had, just like everyone did, but it had never occurred to her she might need anything else.

"Afraid not. Does that mean I'm stuck?"

"Until somebody can get out here in the morning and fix it. You can't drive it the way it is. Where are you headed?"

"My parents' house."

"Come on, I'll give you a lift."

She hesitated, but only for a moment. Whatever reluctance she felt, it would be incredibly foolish to refuse, not to mention rude.

"Wait," she said, "I have to get something from the car."

Before he could respond, she hurried over to the back seat. Jimmy was still fast asleep. He looked very small and vulnerable as only a young child can.

A lump rose in her throat. She lifted him, still wrapped in the blanket and clutching the battered bear. His head fell forward onto her shoulder as he murmured drowsily.

Without looking at Mark, she said, "There's a bag in the front, if you could just get that . . ."

He did so hastily but without taking his eyes from her. By the time she reached the truck, he was there already.

"Here," he said as she started to lift Jimmy, "let me." Gently he took the sleeping boy and laid him on the seat.

Lisa climbed up beside him. Her hands shook slightly as she strapped on the safety belt. She put an arm around Jimmy and held him close as Mark got into the pickup.

He glanced at them both before gunning the engine. "Yours?"

She nodded. "His name is Jimmy. He's four."

"Cute kid. Is your husband going to be visiting, too?"

Her mouth twisted. Mark had always been direct. That, at least, hadn't changed.

"I'm divorced and just for the record, this isn't a visit. I've come to stay."

He looked at her for a long moment before abruptly turning away. The truck moved on through the night.

Silence stretched between them. Lisa cleared her throat. She started to ask how he happened to be out so late, realized how naive that would sound, and changed tack.

"Is hockey season over?"

"Yeah, it is."

"How did you do?"

His mouth twitched. He shot her a sidelong glance. "You follow the game?"

"Well, no, not exactly, but everyone knows you play. Sportscasters talk about you all the time."

His smile deepened. "They haven't had much to say lately. I retired a year ago."

"I've been out of touch," she admitted, thinking that she hadn't realized quite how much. "The last I heard, you were one of the top goalies."

"I did all right," he acknowledged as they turned off the highway onto Langston's main street.

Lisa looked out the window. On the left was the Red Rooster Restaurant where she'd had her first job, waiting tables at sixteen. She'd worked three summers there altogether before going away to college. The tips hadn't been bad.

A little farther down the road and on the opposite side was Marvel's Furniture and Paint Store—"Marvelous Marvel for all your home decorating needs"— actually run by the Marvel family, which was headed by Max and Marian and backed up by their children Martin, Margaret, Miller and—when Marian had finally said "enough already"—Bertrand.

Lisa smiled as she passed it, remembering the white canopy bed her parents had bought for her there, a little girl's dream of a bed covered in dotted swiss and tenderly cherished.

As the road reached toward the center of town the stores were closer together. The Apex Movie Theater was still there—despite the talk that it would either be closed down or taken over by a major chain and transformed into a triplex. One block away was the library and across from that was the elementary school.

The thought flashed through her mind that Jimmy would be going there in a year, starting kindergarten just as she herself had twenty-two years ago. There had been a time when it wouldn't have occurred to her that a child of hers would be following so closely in her footsteps. Now she was simply grateful for the possibility.

Three blocks from the school, on a tree-lined street with deep lawns surrounding well-cared-for houses, the destination that had been in her mind through all the hours and all the miles was at last in front of her. Her parents' house, her childhood home, empty since Nell and Francis Morley had retired to Florida, but still just as she remembered it.

And hers to use on the strength of a single, hurried phone call, no explanations demanded, no questions asked, only the promise that she would tell them if she needed anything else.

Gravel crunched under the wheels as Mark pulled into the driveway. He parked and switched off the ignition. "You all right?" he asked.

She nodded, blinking back the tears that threatened to fall. Relief almost overwhelmed her.

"Go on and open the door," Mark said quietly. "I'll bring the boy."

She picked up her bag, which Mark had placed on the floor, and got out of the truck, fumbling for the right key and unlocking the back door. At once, a flood of familiar sights flowed over her.

Nothing had changed, not the well-scrubbed pine table in the center of the room where she had done her homework, or the rail chairs with their braided cushions, or the cheerful yellow cabinets with glass-paneled doors displaying her mother's china collection.

Correction, she thought with a smile, the refrigerator was new. It was even the kind that dispensed water and ice from a special compartment located on the outside of the door. With all their kids through college and the retirement they had planned so long finally theirs, the Morleys were being good to themselves at last.

It was about time, she thought as the smile faded. They had worked so hard to raise four children well. It didn't seem fair that one of them had managed to stumble so badly.

But she wasn't going to think about that right now. The important thing was to get on with what needed doing. She set the bag down just as Mark walked in with Jimmy.

Her son slept trustingly in his arms. In the quiet of the kitchen, their eyes met. "Where should I put him?" he asked.

"Right here," she said, and went to take him. His small body was warm and strong against her own. "I don't know what we would have done if you hadn't come along," she said and meant it.

He shrugged. "You'd have managed."

The kitchen was spacious, but it had somehow shrunk the moment he'd entered it. Although he made no move to touch her, she felt again the instinctive spurt of fear that she'd experienced back on the highway.

He was so big and hard, and there had always been a wild streak in him. Yet he treated Jimmy with gentleness and, for that matter, herself, as well. The contradiction bewildered her.

Abruptly he said, "You'd better get some sleep."

She nodded and came with him to the door. Softly she said, "Thank you again."

Lisa stood on the back porch until the sound of the pickup died away. All around her, the old familiar world offered itself comfortingly, as though welcoming her back.

But she hardly felt it. All her thoughts were focused on the man who had unexpectedly stepped out of memory to confront her again after so many years.

She didn't want to think about Mark Fletcher. There were enough problems and struggles still ahead of her, the last thing she needed was more. The sooner she put him out of her mind, the better.

Jimmy murmured in his sleep, reminding her of who she was and why she had come. Resolutely she carried the drowsing boy and his battered bear back into the safest place she knew.

Chapter 1

"Don't say no," Jane insisted. "You need to get out." She took another sip of her coffee and grinned. "Besides, it's for a good cause."

Lisa grimaced. She ran a hand through her short, auburn hair. "I'm not really up for a party."

It was a week after the encounter with Mark on the road. In the intervening time, she'd accomplished a great deal—settling into the house, confirming her freelance contracts with various clients she'd worked for in New York, and easing Jimmy's transition into daycare. But she still didn't feel ready to party.

"This is a charity event. The board of education is raising money to buy new computers for the schools. How can you say no, especially since you're in the business?"

"I'm a programmer," Lisa reminded her, "that's all. Besides, you said it was formal."

Jane shrugged. She was a tall, lanky redhead who looked good in anything she wore. Ever since she and Lisa had met way back in kindergarten, it had always been Jane who loved to dress up.

She'd seized any excuse to tote out the spangled evening gowns, feather boas and beaded purses that had been her most prized possessions. Her taste had improved since then, but not by that much.

"Plain" Jane her friends had called her precisely because she was anything but. All these years later, Lisa thought ruefully, and she was still just a tiny bit jealous of Jane, who always seemed to look great and have her act together.

By comparison, Lisa still felt pint-size and bumbling. She was five feet something and well-proportioned, but she yearned for inches in height and in a few other places, too.

That wasn't to be. Compared to glamorous Jane, she was the girl next door—provided you happened to live in a place populated by disgruntled pixies with feathery wisps of hair in their eyes and a certain disinclination to wander out in public.

"I don't want to go," Lisa said.

Jane sighed. She reached for yet another spoonful of sugar to add to her coffee—it was a crime against nature that the woman never gained weight—and said, "I know, but you have to."

"Why?"

"For the same reason you insisted I learn to swim that summer we were both eight. Remember?"

"You'd almost drowned," Lisa said softly. "How could I ever forget?"

"And you said I would drown the next time unless I got back in the water and learned to swim. You hounded me for weeks until I finally agreed."

"I guess I was a little rough on you," Lisa admitted.

Jane's perfectly arched eyebrows shot up. "A little? I seem to recall that I tried to throttle you at one point."

"That was just a little misunderstanding," Lisa insisted. "Besides, you became a pretty good swimmer."

"Because I got back in the water," Jane said. Softly she added, "And you need to do the same."

"I haven't exactly had a close encounter with a lungful of chlorine," Lisa said quietly. She looked down at the table. "Chas was a little more than that."

"He was a bastard," Jane said emphatically. "A gorgeous, sexy, rich bastard. The only good thing he ever did was father Jimmy and he couldn't even do that right. But you're rid of him, pal. The only problem is you don't seem to realize it."

"I did," Lisa murmured. "We've been divorced for almost four years. The only contact we have is through our lawyers and even that isn't much. I was getting on with my life, everything was fine and then . . ."

"Then what?" Jane asked quietly. She put her hand over her friend's. "I haven't wanted to push, but it's pretty obvious something sent you back here in a big hurry. I thought you liked New York?"

Lisa shrugged. She glanced out the window to where Jimmy was playing in the backyard. In the week since their arrival, he'd already made friends with several of the neighborhood children.

Freed from the confines of a city apartment, he seemed to be having the time of his life. She was grateful for that, but she couldn't shake the uneasy sense that nothing was ever this simple.

"I did like it for a while," she said, her eyes still on Jimmy. "It was an exciting, vibrant place and when I met Chas, everything seemed perfect. But later, being on my own with Jimmy, I started to wonder if it was the right place to bring him up. Then the . . . problems started."

"What problems?" Jane asked.

Lisa sighed. She stood up and went over to the counter to pour herself another cup of coffee. Her hands shook slightly.

"Phone calls, to begin with," she said. "They came at all hours of the day and night as though someone was trying to find out when I was home. Then the woman who baby-sat for me said she thought someone was following her when she took Jimmy to the park. I didn't put much store in it since everyone tends to get a little paranoid after a while, but then it started happening with me."

She sat down again at the table but made no effort to drink the coffee. More caffeine wasn't what she needed.

"It got so I was afraid to go anywhere. That's when I started working at home. But the worst part was that I didn't want to let Jimmy out of my sight. He's just a little boy. He's got to have as normal a life as possible, even if I couldn't manage to give him a decent father."

"So you came here," Jane said quietly.

Lisa nodded. "I couldn't think of anywhere else. I can work, Jimmy can make friends. We'll be all right."

Jane looked at her steadily. She said nothing, just looked, until she seemed to come to a decision in her own mind. Briskly she stood up and took her cup over to the sink.

Over her shoulder, she said, "Lisa Morley, you come with me tomorrow night or we won't be friends anymore, pinky swear."

"Yeah, right."

"I mean it. You were always the bravest person I ever knew." At Lisa's surprised look, she went on. "Yes, you were. You went off to college and the big city with wings on your feet. You got married, had a child and went it alone while the rest of us were still trying to figure out what we wanted out of life. You've got guts, kid, and I'm not about to let you forget it."

"It's not a big deal," Lisa said. "I'll send a check."

"Oh, no, you won't. You'll put on your best kick-heels dress and give this town something to talk about."

Lisa hesitated. Her friend looked serious and the more she thought about it, the more she had to agree. She'd had it with hiding and running. She was home now and by heaven, she was going to act like it.

The corners of her mouth trembled suspiciously. "There's just one problem."

"What?"

"I don't happen to have a kick-heels dress."

Jane grinned, the battle won. "You came to the right place, kid. I'll get you fixed up in no time."

"With a dress," Lisa admonished. "Just a dress. Right?"

"Yeah, sure," Jane said airily. "A dress. What did you think I meant?"

"Nothing, I didn't think you meant anything."

"A man, maybe. A real, honest-to-goodness, grown-up man? Not just a gorgeous hunk in a suit?"

"There are no real men," Lisa said matter-of-factly. "There are only other women's husbands, gentlemen of another persuasion and guys like Chas."

Jane's eyes twinkled but she said nothing more on the subject, and after a while, Lisa forgot about it.

One day later—dressed in a white silk sheath that hugged her slender frame and somehow also managed to make her look taller—she remembered. But by then it was too late.

Chapter 2

The high school gym was packed. Lisa stood just inside the entrance and looked around. She felt as though she had stepped back in time.

Banners covered the walls, streamers hung from the ceiling, colored lights revolved and a purple-tuxedoed band was banging out vintage tunes for the appreciative crowd. She caught sight of half a dozen people she recognized right away and there was no question she'd find more. It seemed as though everyone in Langston had turned out for the event.

Jane gave her an encouraging grin and promptly vanished. Lisa hadn't bargained on that. She started to go after her friend, hesitated, and ended up standing awkwardly off to one side.

She'd been wrong to think nothing had changed. Back in high school, she'd been one of the bright, successful girls, part of a closely knit clique that went to everything together and whose members were always on hand to lend moral support. She couldn't remember ever feeling like an outsider. But she did now.

Watching the couples swirling by, laughing and talking with the ease of long acquaintance, she felt like a spectator at a party where she didn't belong. Self-consciousness swept over her. She glanced toward the door.

"Going somewhere?" a deep masculine voice inquired.

Startled, Lisa turned too quickly. She teetered and almost lost her balance on the four-inch heels Jane had insisted she wear. A strong, bronzed hand reached out to steady her.

"Easy," Mark said.

She flushed and pulled her arm away. For just an instant she had a vivid sense of his strength and how easily he could have held on to her, but he released her immediately. Light blue eyes met hers.

Lisa realized she was staring and tried to stop, but not with any great success.

The roughly dressed stranger of several nights before was gone. In his place was a man of austere elegance, the last word in masculine sophistication. The difference was startling and yet, as she looked further, she realized he wasn't so different after all.

The evening clothes did nothing to disguise the massive sweep of his shoulders and chest or the tapered strength of narrow hips and powerful thighs. Just standing there, under the revolving colored lights in the noisy gym, he exuded quiet strength and barely contained power.

His gaze ran down her slender body to the hem of her abbreviated skirt and the tapered legs below. Although he was standing several feet away from her, she felt his touch as though it were a physical presence, stroking her boldly and without compunction.

"I'm going to take a guess that Jane MacEnroe had something to do with that dress," he said, and smiled.

Lisa blinked, startled by his perceptiveness. "How did you know that?"

"Because the two of you were good friends and it looks more to her taste than the kind of thing you usually wore."

"Does that mean you don't like it?" Lisa asked. Her sudden boldness surprised her. Why on earth would she ask that? Whether he liked it or not didn't concern her at all.

Or at least it shouldn't have.

His eyes touched her again. She watched, unwillingly fascinated, as his hard mouth softened into a seductive smile. "Oh, I like it all right," he said.

She was working on an answer to that when a new rush of people jostled past them.

"If you stay here," Mark said, "you're going to get trampled. How about a drink?"

"All right," Lisa replied cautiously. Alarm bells were going off in her head. All the secret, furtive thoughts she'd had about Mark Fletcher way back when were returning with a vengeance.

Worse yet, she was vulnerable in a way she hadn't been then and she knew it. If she had any sense, she'd turn right around and put as much distance between them as she could manage.

Only two things stopped her. The first was that she realized right then and there that she'd had it with running. The second was that she wanted to go with him.

She took a deep breath, threw caution to the wind, and followed. His hand, holding hers, was warm and solid. His touch was firm but also gentle. It sent little bolts of electricity through her, which she did her very best to ignore.

Several people glanced at them with frank interest as they passed. They reached the bar set up along one wall of the gym.

"What will you have?" Mark asked.

"A white wine spritzer," Lisa replied. She waited, expecting him to ask for a beer, but instead he surprised her.

"Spritzer and an iced tea," he said. When the drinks were ready, he paid the bartender and handed Lisa her glass.

She glanced at the one he still held. Before she could stop herself, she said, "You've changed."

"Life has a way of doing that to you," he said and took a sip. Over the rim of the glass his eyes met hers. Softly he added, "You've changed, too."

She hesitated, not sure of what to say. Unbidden, an image of herself in high school flashed through her mind. She'd been practically a straight *A* student, co-president of the debating club and a cheerleader.

Everything she'd tried, she'd succeeded at. Moreover, she'd done it almost effortlessly, or at least it had seemed that way. Not too surprisingly, she had simply presumed that life would continue along the same track.

Instead, she'd been derailed.

"It's had its ups and downs," she admitted and, before she could stop herself, returned his smile. There was something about standing there with him, just talking, something so real and solid that it almost scared her. At least, if she'd been thinking straight, it would have.

The area right in front of the bar was getting busier. Before she could object, he took her arm and steered her off to the side, further into the shadows at the edge of the gym.

She shouldn't stay with him, she knew that. She should tell him she had friends to join, and then leave. Mark Fletcher was everything she'd promised herself she'd avoid—a dangerous, willful man who lived life on the edge. She was crazy to have anything to do with him.

Yet there she was, so close that she could feel the warmth of his big, hard body and see the hard, unrelenting gleam of his eyes. Instinctively, thinking of the boy he had been, she glanced at the glass in his hand.

"I gave up alcohol a long time before I quit hockey," he said quietly.

"There was an accident," she murmured, suddenly remembering. Her mother had written her something about it while she was away at college. Mark had been playing hockey in Vancouver. He'd been alone in his car when it took a turn too sharply, went off the highway and ended up wrapped around a tree. The police had estimated he'd been doing at least ninety miles per hour at the time, maybe more, and he'd been legally drunk.

"Nobody else got hurt," he said. "That was the only good part. I spent two months in the hospital thinking about what I could have done to another person. It was enough."

She nodded slowly. Her first instinct about him had been right, this definitely wasn't the boy she'd known in high school. In front of her was a man who had been through tough and even terrifying times, and who had triumphed over them.

An honest-to-goodness, grown-up man who also happened to make her insides feel like melted butter. Just what she definitely didn't need at this point in her life.

And yet...it felt so damn good to be standing there with him. So damn right.

She'd been alone for so long. All her intelligence and energy had gone into being a good mother for Jimmy, trying to make up to him for the lack of a father.

The struggle to do that had kept her from coming to terms with how angry and abandoned she felt. Chas had done more than rob Jimmy of a needed parent. He'd stolen Lisa's confidence in herself as a woman.

She hadn't wanted to admit that even to herself, but standing there in her old high school gym, looking up at Mark, she had no choice. Either she could go off and lick her wounds, or she could acknowledge that this was a new beginning for her and she had better act the part.

Her back straightened. She lifted her head and met the clear blue eyes that were studying her so closely.

The band was playing a slow tune. Music drifted over the crowd. Mark set his glass down on the table behind him. Holding her gaze, he asked, "Would you like to dance?"

She took a deep breath, put her own glass on a table and nodded.

Chapter 3

She felt so good in his arms. The realization of that went through Mark like a bolt. He held her with almost exaggerated care, more mindful of his own strength than he could ever remember being.

Not that she was fragile, far from it. She had the well-honed skin and easy grace of a woman in excellent condition. But more than that, she had courage. He'd seen it in her eyes when she'd said that she was staying.

Something had hurt her. He'd seen that, too, and the knowledge created a hard knot of anger deep inside him. Ten years ago she'd been a confident, carefree girl he'd looked at with mingled lust and envy.

Now she was a woman—older, wiser, maybe even a little frayed around the edges. A *real* woman, not some tuck-here, nip-there, walking, talking mannequin with no one home inside. Real.

She even smelled real—like a field of wildflowers on a warm summer's day. The scent of wind was in her hair. He closed his eyes for a moment and felt his senses swim.

This was crazy. He was just getting his life straightened out. Things were going good. It was no time to rock the boat. If his ex-wife had taught him anything, it was that women and trouble were one and the same. He didn't want either.

Or at least he hadn't when he'd walked into the gym. Now he had to think again. Seeing Lisa Morley—especially the grown-up version—was more than he'd bargained on. But it was a party, after all, and a couple of dances couldn't do any harm. It was all strictly casual.

A slender, pleasant-looking man approached. He gave Lisa a warm smile. "Mind if I cut in?"

Before Lisa could respond, Mark drew his brows together and shot the interloper one of those glances that men have been giving each other since longer than anybody knows. "Yeah," he said, "I do."

The man backed off hastily. Mark hardly noticed. All his attention was focused on the woman who had suddenly stiffened in his arms.

"That was rude," she said.

He sighed. So much for casual. "I know, and I apologize. Something came over me."

She hesitated. Although they continued to dance, he could feel her uncertainty. It wasn't hard to understand. She wouldn't have been a woman if she hadn't been at least a little flattered by his possessiveness.

Yet it also increased her wariness. He had a sudden, fleeting image of a proud doe cautiously lifting her head to sniff the air and smiled at his own imagination. It didn't usually run along such romantic lines.

"Don't worry," he said quietly, "I'm not usually this Neanderthal."

To his relief, she smiled. "Actually, they got a bum rap. Neanderthal culture was pretty advanced."

"That's right, you were always interested in the past. What did you do, become an anthropologist?"

She shook her head. "Wrong direction. I went for computers, specifically artificial intelligence."

"Find any?" he asked.

"Not so far, but we're still looking. In the meantime, I write software."

"Oh, yeah? What language?"

When she told him, he said, "We just put in a new system at work using that. It was a little hairy at first, but I think we've gotten most of the kinks out."

Lisa sighed. Here she was, in the arms of the man she had always secretly desired, and what were they talking about? Computers, of course.

He heard the sigh and laughed. "Don't worry. That's the last I'll say about it."

"It's all right," she said softly. "I don't mind talking about work."

"It's a safe topic, isn't it?"

She looked up, straight into his eyes. "You don't pull your punches, do you?"

He shook his head. "Never have. What brought you back from New York?"

She hesitated. They were moving effortlessly, as though they had danced together many times before. His hand was warm against her back. She felt surrounded by strength but also by a steely resolve that would not be denied.

Mark Fletcher was a tough man. He'd had to be to get where he was and, moreover, arrive there in one piece. He wasn't going to be satisfied with half-truths or evasions.

So be it. She wasn't fond of either of those herself. But she did value her privacy and she wasn't about to expose more of her feelings than she felt safe revealing.

"I thought it would be better to raise Jimmy here rather than in the city." It was true so far as it went. For the moment that would have to be enough.

Mark frowned. He sensed there was a good deal more she wasn't saying, but he also suspected that there'd be nothing gained by pressing her. She had stiffened again in his arms, just after she'd been beginning to relax.

Something about her son put her very much on guard. He felt anger for the unknown man who had created a child with her but who wasn't there to help raise him.

"Divorce is rough," he said quietly.

Her eyes widened. "You, too?"

He shrugged. "'Fraid so. At least in my case there weren't any kids involved."

Or much of anything else, he thought. Once his ex-wife heard that he didn't give a flying rhymes-with-puck who got the wedding silver and china, the furniture or the condo in Florida, she'd been only too happy to sign on the dotted line. The mere fact that he hadn't cared—not even a little—told him that the marriage had been over long before he'd walked out the door.

"I guess that does make it easier," Lisa murmured. The music had ended, catching them both unaware.

Mark stepped back but not very far. Around them, the party went on. People were laughing and a few had begun singing old songs. But it seemed to be happening to other people, not to them. They were apart, separate from everything else. Alone.

On impulse, he bent his head. Her head was up-turned toward him. It required only the barest effort for his mouth to brush hers.

Her lips were full, smooth and warm. They parted slightly in surprise beneath his own. Desire roared through him. For an instant, it was all he could do not to take her into his arms.

But the iron-clad discipline that had carried him so far through life stopped him. It was too soon, she was too wary.

"Have you had dinner yet?" he asked.

Lisa shook her head, hardly aware that she did so. The kiss had been so brief that she almost thought she had imagined it. Only the tingling bursts of pleasure coursing through her told her it had been very real.

Coming back to earth, she looked around her. A buffet was being set up off to one side of the gym, but she'd had little appetite when she'd left the house and really hadn't expected to eat.

Her stomach, though, had other ideas. It rumbled just as the party seemed to close in around her, leaving her with no thought except to get away.

"How about the Rooster?" Mark asked with a wry smile. He, too, was surprised by his sudden hunger.

There were at least a dozen reasons why she should say no, Lisa thought. It was just too bad that she couldn't seem to remember any of them.

Instead she nodded and looked around for Jane, intending to tell her that she was going. As it turned out, she didn't have to. Her friend caught her eye from clear across the gym and grinned knowingly, just as though she'd planned the whole thing.

"I should have known," Lisa muttered under her breath.

"What's that?" Mark asked as he steered a path for them through the crowd.

"Pay no attention. I frequently talk to myself."

"Any other little habits I ought to know about?"

"Just the baying at the moon thing, but it's not a big deal. How about you?"

He shook his head. "It's embarrassing how boring I am."

Lisa shot him a sidelong glance from beneath her lashes. He stood, tall and powerful, just beyond the entrance to the gym. As she watched, he loosened his tie absently and undid the top button of his shirt, exposing the thickly muscled column of his throat.

Right, she thought, boring was the word she would have picked, too. In two, maybe three million years.

The parking valet caught his eye, nodded and trotted off. Moments later he returned. Lisa's breath caught in her throat. It couldn't be . . . could it?

"A Mustang?" she asked, almost reverently. And a red one to boot, gleaming with the luster of a thousand coats of wax—each lovingly applied—whitewalls sparkling, chrome unmarred by the tiniest imperfection. A thing of beauty.

"Nineteen sixty-seven," Mark said, his pride admirably restrained. "Some people prefer the sixty-nine, but I still think sixty-seven has the edge."

"You're a car man," she said, somewhat unnecessarily.

"Guilty. I also like football, eat steak, enjoy riding a tractor and find any excuse I can to go fishing. When you get right down to it, I'm practically a cliché."

"Practically?" Lisa asked with a grin. She was feeling oddly light-headed, as though she had suddenly stepped out of her own life and into another, one without the problems and fears that had weighed her down for so long.

He held the passenger door open for her, waited while she got in, and shut it. When he was settled beside her, he said, "Okay, you've got me, totally."

"Why don't I believe you?"

"Maybe you're just naturally suspicious?"

"Who told you that?" she demanded with mock sternness.

He laughed and gunned the engine. The bright lights around the gym faded behind them. They were out on the road, heading for the restaurant. It was too cool an evening to put the top down.

Lisa found herself regretting that. Riding in a classic Mustang was something she realized belatedly that she'd always wanted to do. This might be the only chance she'd ever get. It was a shame not to do it right.

"What're you thinking?" Mark asked. He'd caught the small furrow between her brows.

"You'll laugh."

"Tell me, anyway."

"I was thinking if you're going to ride around in a Mustang, you really ought to have the top down."

"Fine by me, but aren't you going to feel a little chilly?"

"It's a dumb idea," she admitted.

"No," he said, "it isn't." Holding the wheel with one hand, he stripped off his jacket and tossed it to her. "Here, put this on."

"I can't take your jacket," she protested.

"In about two minutes, the temperature's going to fall twenty degrees. That little whatchamacallit you're wearing isn't exactly insulated."

She took the hint, and the jacket. The dark wool was smooth beneath her fingers. It was far too large, enveloping her so that she felt wrapped in warmth and comfort. A slight scent clung to the fine fabric—soap and leather mingling with the fragrance of the night air.

She sighed and shut her eyes as a sense of security so intense that it all but took her breath away swept over her.

It was false, of course. She had to remember that. Such security was for children fortunate enough to be deeply loved and protected. It was even for naive young women who thought themselves better able to cope with the world than they really were.

It wasn't for her, not after all she had experienced. For her, it was enough to know that she had gotten this far and achieved this much.

Jimmy slept happily in her old room, watched over by Jane's mother, who had been more than willing to baby-sit. When he woke, the sun would be shining and the birds singing, all would be right with his world.

She loved her son to the very depths of her being, but just then, for just a moment, she envied him. She had just about reconciled herself to the fact that for her nothing would ever be that completely perfect again.

Just about, but not quite.

She turned her head slightly to look at Mark. In profile, the rugged harshness of his features stood out starkly.

The pretty, male attractiveness that graced the glossy pictures of fashion magazines and TV and movie screens was completely missing in him. He possessed a raw, masculine strength redolent of a far more primitive time, when men had ruled by the sheer power of their will, enduring every hardship and danger to protect what belonged to them.

Not that it mattered. She was immune. Chas had cured her once and for all of any interest in the male gender. She had her child and her work, in time she might take up knitting, perhaps make a quilt, get a cat. The possibilities were endless.

"Warm enough?" Mark asked as they sped through the night, the wind blowing holes through old notions.

She nodded but still drew his jacket more closely around her as she tried to figure out how this man out of her past had managed to make the present look so suddenly and startlingly different.

Chapter 4

The Red Rooster was almost empty when they got there. Most everyone had gone to the fund-raiser. A young, bored-looking waitress perked up when she saw Lisa and Mark.

They had their choice of tables and picked one by the windows overlooking the river that ran behind the building. It was a pretty, tranquil setting even at night, when the water had to be more imagined than actually seen.

"Do you come here often?" Lisa asked when the waitress had taken their orders. Seated across the table from Mark in the shadowed, hushed room, she felt a quiver of nervousness. There was no getting around it, he was a compelling man.

As a teenager, he'd possessed that keen knifelike edge of danger that inevitably drew the innocent, herself included. Now it was gone.

In its place was the toughness she'd noticed earlier, but also much more, an ability to laugh at himself, for instance, and even to apologize when he knew he'd done something wrong as he had when he'd been rude to the man who'd tried to cut in on their dance.

Those were all sterling qualities, but they made her even more wary. She simply couldn't afford to be hurt again.

"Not very," Mark said. He was watching her with equal care. She sensed some of the same wariness in him that she felt in herself. "The business takes up most of my time," he added.

She nodded, trying to seem as though she understood when in fact she didn't. Honesty won out over the distant courtesy of strangers. It might have been safer had it not, but the simple fact was that she didn't feel like a stranger. Far from it.

"About that," she said, "it's another change for you, isn't it?"

He raised an eyebrow slightly. "How do you mean?"

She flushed, thinking that she should have guessed he wouldn't make it easy. They were both being so very careful. "Only that you loved hockey in high school, it was the one thing you seemed to really enjoy other than . . ." Her color deepened. She'd put her foot right in it.

"Girls?" he asked deadpan. "Hockey and girls, is that what you mean?"

"And motorcycles," she added. Let him get the better of her if he could. She wasn't backing off now.

"True enough," he admitted with a laugh. "What's the point?"

She ignored the curling heat in her stomach his smile evoked and went on. "That no one was surprised when you turned pro. Thrilled, sure, but not surprised. But this thing with the agribusiness. What made you decide that you wanted to go into farming?"

He hesitated, swirling the iced tea in his glass unseeingly. Finally he said, "My dad was a farmer, did you know that?"

She nodded slowly. Bob Fletcher was a dim figure she'd glimpsed around town only rarely. Somewhere she'd gotten the impression that he drank much and prospered little.

There'd been no wife for Bob Fletcher, no mother for Mark. Rumor had it that she'd run off when he was a small child, leaving father and son to work things out between them as best they could.

"I guess I heard that," she said tentatively.

"Yeah, I'll bet you did. My old man was a mean SOB on a good day. When he wasn't feeling right with the world, you had to be real stupid to go anywhere near him."

Her throat tightened. She had a sudden, too vivid glimpse of the childhood he'd had. It hurt more than she wanted to admit.

Years ago, she hadn't thought of such things. But since Jimmy had come along, she seemed to see everything more clearly, even when it wasn't too pretty to look at.

"So you stayed away..."

He shrugged as though it was nothing of importance, just the usual routine of life. "I played hockey. Found it by accident when I was three and slid out on the ice behind our house. Lucky it was frozen solid or I'd have gone right through."

He lifted his glass, as though toasting the past. She stole a quick glance into his eyes and saw to her relief that the smile was there, too. It fit with the man she'd already seen, a man who had the past—and its pain—in clear perspective.

"What happened to your dad?" she asked, feeling safer about asking him than she would have before.

"His liver gave out," Mark said softly. "He knew he was dying and he wrote me a letter, only one he ever wrote in his life. Told me a lot of stuff, most of it I'd kind of known. But the thing that really struck me was that he said the happiest he'd been was when he could watch something grow. It was the only time he said he had any peace. Up until then, I'd pretty much decided anything he did, I ought to do the opposite. But that got me to thinking. It turned out we weren't so different after all, at least not in some ways."

"So you came back?" she asked softly.

He nodded. "Remember Ben Harris?"

"Sure, he and my dad were friends." The Harrises had run one of the bigger spreads outside of town, but she seemed to remember that their kids had gone on to other things.

"He wanted to retire down to the Carolinas where his daughter is. We cut a deal and that was that."

"Goodbye hockey, hello farming? I still say it was a big change. How do you like it?"

"Depends," he said wryly. "When I crawl out of bed before dawn with it pouring down rain and my knees reminding me of how many body slams I took, I think I must be nuts. But we planted two hundred acres a few weeks ago. There's a lot of satisfaction in that.''

"I know what you mean," she said quietly. "When I look at Jimmy, I feel the same way."

The waitress returned with their orders. When she was gone, Mark said, "It must be hard, raising a kid on your own."

She thought of all the sleepless nights, the worry and exhaustion, the constant effort and unrelenting care. And then thought of too, the smiles and hugs, the first steps and words, the incandescent sense of the world seen again for the first time through a child's eyes.

Firmly she said, "It's worth it."

"Still, you must have some help. Your ex—"

"Is mountain climbing in the Himalayas or shooting the rapids in the Amazon or maybe dog sledding across Antarctica. I gave up trying to keep track of him a long time ago."

"He doesn't see Jimmy?"

"Not in almost two years and before then he wasn't exactly a frequent visitor in our lives." She spoke as lightly as she could, but some of the tension she felt crept into her voice. "Chas isn't my favorite topic of conversation," she admitted.

"Chas?" Mark repeated with a note of disbelief. "What kind of name is that?"

"Uppercrust WASP," she said ruefully. "Old New England money, the whole nine yards. It's short for Charles Albert David Howell. Not too many people know this, but when the pilgrims on the *Mayflower* got here, the first thing they saw was a Howell down on the beach pounding a Members Only sign into the sand. That's how long they've been here."

Mark shook his head in mock dismay. "How did you get hooked up with a guy like that?"

"Just lucky, I guess. Chas was great to be with until he found out Jimmy was on the way. Then he decided he wasn't cut out for the home and hearth routine. We had a terribly civilized divorce, probably the only one on record, and went our separate ways."

An ominous look flashed behind Mark's light blue eyes. "Am I getting this straight, he left you while you were pregnant?"

"You think he should have hung around until Jimmy was born and then left? Or maybe stayed even longer and made us all miserable? No, thanks. Once I realized how he felt, I was just as glad to see the back of him."

He shook his head ruefully. "Do you happen to know anyone these days who has a good marriage?"

"My folks, some of their friends . . ." She stopped, thinking hard. She'd known a lot of people back in New York, at least at the passing acquaintance level.

Maybe some of them had been happily married and she just hadn't heard about it. But the people she'd known best had either never married or were divorced.

"Marriage just isn't what it used to be," she said with a sigh. "The truth is, maybe it never was, except for the lucky few."

"That sounds pretty cynical for a former cheerleader."

She rolled her eyes. "Please, there are some things about my past I'm trying to live down. Anyway, it's true. People used to have their marriages arranged for them. They only got married for material benefit and to protect their children. Nobody expected to be wildly in love or have their every need satisfied by marriage. It was more of a business relationship than anything else."

"And you think that's good?"

"I think it couldn't have been any worse than what we've got now. Let me ask you, why did you get married?"

He looked taken aback by the question. A dark stain spread over his lean cheeks. "Would you believe I can't remember?"

"Nope," she said flatly, "you've got to have some idea."

"First, you tell me why you married *Chaass.*"

The way he ran the name out made Lisa laugh. "Some kind of hormonal imbalance, I think, triggered by excessive starry-eyedness. Your turn."

"Kind of the same. In the back of my mind, I think I had some idea about settling down, building something permanent, that kind of thing. I was tired of life on the road, the groupies, all that."

She looked skeptical. "You were?"

"Yeah, believe it or not, I was. Besides, the world's changed. Even if you want to be irresponsible, you've got to know you could be putting your life on the line."

"I must have missed something," Lisa said. "Chas looked like Mr. Respectability—right family, right school, right tie, the whole bit. But he runs off to climb mountains while Wild Mark Fletcher turns straight arrow. Did we go through some kind of time-space warp?"

"Could be," he said softly. "What happened to the cheerleader with all the hair who never mussed her manicure and looked like she'd slide through life without a wrinkle?"

"I traded her in on a more up-to-date model." She took a bite of the chicken she'd ordered but hardly tasted it. He was too distracting by half, this disarmingly honest man who cared about permanency and responsibility.

She wasn't ready for this, didn't even believe in it anymore. When Chas left, he'd taken her belief in that kind of commitment with him.

But life went on. Didn't the mere fact that she was sitting there in the Red Rooster opposite Wild Mark Fletcher prove it? They were both survivors of the big letdown.

The only question was, what were they going to do about it?

Chapter 5

#include "stdio.h", Lisa typed, *#include "stdlib.h"*

She was working in the big sunlit room her father had used as a den. Her computer was set up on the desk, the screen lit and the hard disk humming.

Jimmy was at the play group she'd enrolled him in. He'd loved it from the first moment and was ready to race out the door every morning to get there.

The group was run by Jane's mother, who had also made it clear she would love to do more baby-sitting for Lisa. So far, the need hadn't come up.

She was hard at work on a free-lance programming job and glad to be so. Being busy kept her from thinking too much.

FILE *fp;
int i, num[
No, that was wrong. She backspaced and typed *m;*

It had been a week since she'd seen Mark. Once, when she was out shopping, she thought she'd caught a glimpse of his pickup truck, but she wasn't sure.

Not that it mattered. Jimmy was happy, she had her work, it was enough. Except that she had to remind herself of that several times a day.

The phone rang. She broke off what she was doing and reached for it.

"Hello?"

"Miss Morley? It's Fred, at your building. You called while I was out?"

Fred Baker was the superintendent of the apartment house in New York where she and Jimmy had lived. He was an ex-Marine and retired cop who had seen six kids through college and took no grief from anyone. Lisa had chosen the building—at least in part—because of his presence.

"Thanks for calling back," she said. "How are you?"

"Just fine, and yourself?"

"Good, thanks." The pleasantries out of the way, she got down to it. "I realize this is short notice, Mr. Baker, but Jimmy and I are moving out. I've sent the last month's rent in already. The movers will be there first thing next week."

She'd left in such a hurry that there'd been no time to take anything except Jimmy's dearly loved toys and books. For herself, she'd brought only her computer and a few clothes. Everything else would have to follow.

"Mrs. Harris, the lady who baby-sat for me, is coming in to supervise the packing. She has a key, so you don't need to be there, but I didn't want you to be surprised.''

There was silence for a moment before Fred Baker said, "I'm surprised, anyway, Miss Morley. This is awful sudden, isn't it?"

Fred had always gone out of his way to be kind to her and Jimmy. He deserved an explanation.

"Yes," she agreed, "it is. But we were having some trouble getting along in the city and I thought we'd be better off back home."

"I can understand that," the older man said. "This can be a tough place."

He was silent again, thinking, then he said, "But I got a feeling there's more to it than that. This have anything to do with the men who have been hanging around here the last few days?"

Lisa inhaled sharply. The fear she'd come to feel in the city had been strong enough to send her running, but it had also been nebulous and ill-defined. She hadn't known for sure if there was really anything to be afraid of or not.

"What men?" she asked faintly.

"Three of them," Baker answered promptly, "working shifts round the clock. They drive late-model cars and dress good but not flashy. They're not cops or I'd know about it. My guess is they're private investigators."

He paused, giving her a chance to jump in. When she didn't, he went on. "We've got one hundred and twenty tenants in this building, not counting over-night guests. I can think of ten, maybe fifteen of them somebody might want to keep an eye on. But three P.I.s doing twenty-four-hour-a-day surveillance is expensive. It's a little past the usual matrimonial action, know what I mean?''

"Have they questioned anyone?" Lisa asked. "The doormen? You?"

Her mind was racing. It might be that the men had nothing to do with her, but the mention of what they must be costing made her fear the worst. Chas hadn't been top heavy in the honor and decency department, but he'd had no shortage of money.

"Nope," Fred Baker said, "which is unusual by itself. But there's no doubt they're watching the building. Hymie Gonzalez, the night doorman, said he caught one of them taking pictures."

"Of what?"

"The front windows. You know you left your blinds down? After this many days, it's pretty clear you're not there."

"I guess it will be even clearer when they see my stuff being moved out," she said. Her throat was so tight that it hurt. What on earth was going on?

"That's why I mentioned it. Will the movers have your new address?"

"Yes," Lisa murmured. "They'd have to."

"Listen," Mr. Baker said quickly when he heard the fear in her voice, "I've got a suggestion. Why don't you just tell me what you really have to have and I'll pack it. I can send it by regular mail. If we act fast enough, they won't realize what we're doing until it's too late. The rest of the stuff can stay in storage right here in the basement. That way nobody will have to know your address except me, and believe me, Miss Morley, I'm too old a nut to crack."

"It's very kind of you," Lisa began. Not for the first time, she was struck by the fact that even in a town as tough as New York, there were genuinely kind people. "But..."

"I also don't scare easy, if that's what you're thinking. My oldest daughter had trouble with her exhusband. It nearly broke my heart the hell he put her through. I didn't find out about it until she'd suffered by herself way too long. I don't want to think something like that could happen to anybody I know while I just stood by and let it."

Lisa's hand tightened on the receiver. "What makes you think my ex-husband is involved with this?" For that matter, how had he figured out that she'd been divorced?

"When you moved in here," Fred Baker said matter-of-factly, "you still had marks on your ring finger, so I figured you'd been married until a short time before. You get mail addressed to both Morley and Howell, so you must have gone back to your maiden name at some point but not everybody is using it. You've got a wonderful boy, but there's no sign of any daddy showing up for visitation."

He paused. "I can't see you keeping a decent man from his child, so something's not right. Then those men show up just as you hottail it out of here. Maybe I'm reading too much into all this and if I am, you just say so. But from where I sit, it looks a lot like what went on with my daughter."

"Mr. Baker," Lisa said softly.

"Yes?"

"Would you just answer one question for me? How is it you didn't make detective?"

He laughed. "Never was any good at paperwork. So am I right?"

"Close enough. I'm sorry your daughter had a bad time, but I do appreciate your help."

"Think nothing of it. Now you just tell me what you need and I'll take care of the rest."

Half an hour later, Lisa hung up the phone. She sat for a time staring out the window. Spring was coming late, fighting a stubborn winter, but the daffodils were poking their heads up and buds were swelling on the magnolia trees. More than ever, Langston seemed an oasis of peace and safety.

If Fred Baker hadn't been so sharp, if he hadn't come to the right conclusions and called her in time, if she'd gone ahead with her plans and had her belongings sent . . .

A shudder ran through her. If her fears were right, and someone *had* been watching her and Jimmy, then everything she'd done so far would have been useless. They'd have known right where she was.

But to what end? She had lived in the same apartment since before Jimmy was born. At no time had she made a secret of her whereabouts or tried to conceal her movements. She'd been right there for anyone who wanted to reach her.

Why was it only now that she felt so threatened? Nothing had really changed, at least so far as she knew.

But then she knew very little. Her marriage to Chas had been so brief that she'd never met any of his family. They'd spoken their vows at city hall—much to the dismay of her parents—honeymooned in the Caribbean, and jumped right back into their busy lives.

Eighteen months later, she was pregnant and he was gone. He hadn't reacted when she informed him by letter that she wanted a divorce and the termination of their marriage. He'd let the lawyers take care of everything.

She could have been a rich woman, she thought with a humorless smile. She could still remember her own lawyer's disbelief when she'd refused to take anything for herself.

Chas did help to support Jimmy and, to give him credit, he'd never missed a payment. But then they, too, went through his attorneys. He didn't even have to write a check.

Which brought her straight back to her original question: why was this happening now?

Or was it?

There was still a possibility that the phone calls had been a coincidence and that Mrs. Harris had been imagining things when she said she believed someone was following her and Jimmy. There might be no connection at all to the men watching the apartment house.

But it still paid to be on the safe side. She'd come all the way back to Langston for just that reason and she didn't intend to budge another inch. Whatever trouble might be brewing, she could face it better there than any other place in the world.

She looked back at the computer screen. Automatically she typed *if (fp =fopen ("rand", "rb")) = =NULL) {*

The characters flickered at her meaninglessly. She had lost the train of her thought. At that moment she couldn't even remember what the subroutine was supposed to be for.

Disgusted, she turned the screen off and glanced at the clock. There were still a couple of hours before she was due to pick Jimmy up. Maybe a drive would clear her head.

She locked the door behind her, got into the car and headed out of town without giving any thought to what direction she took.

Chapter 6

The rail fence ran along the left side of the road, over soft hillocks of greening earth, past proud old oak trees, stopping once or twice for a side-cut dirt road leading off out of sight, but picking up again, on and on until even the most unobservant person had to take notice.

Lisa watched the fence flick past out of the corner of her eye. She eased up on the accelerator and glanced at the dashboard clock. She was half an hour out of Langston, traveling a road she had known in childhood but along which she'd no conscious intent of driving.

But then again, she'd left the house with no clear plans for going anywhere. Could she really claim to be so surprised that she had ended up here, along the outer boundaries of what had, in times gone by, been the Harris place?

She could stop and turn around easily enough. There was nothing to say she had to keep going. Stop, turn, go back to town, get a little more work done before picking up Jimmy. That was what she ought to do.

She kept going.

The farm was bigger than even she had remembered. It stretched on seemingly forever, dotted here and there with equipment sheds, silos and barns.

Everything she saw was meticulously maintained, there was no sign of slackness anywhere. Ben Harris had run a tight ship and apparently Mark was doing the same.

Finally she pulled over to the side of the road and sat for a while staring into space. It was a spectacular day, the sky washed a brilliant blue and a crisp breeze blowing from the north. A day to blow the cobwebs out of the mind and energize the spirit.

She leaned back against the seat and closed her eyes. Since coming home to Langston, she had certainly been sleeping better than she had in New York, but her sleep was tangled up with dreams that woke her sometimes, eyes wide and heart racing, torn between wrenching fear and sweet longing. A shrink would have had a field day, she thought with a drowsy grin.

The windows of the car were down. Sun-drenched air touched her skin lightly. She could hear the soft hum of insects and much farther away, out across the fields, the low rumble of a tractor churning the rich black earth.

If she hadn't had to pick up Jimmy, she might easily have drifted into sleep. But the memory of that lingered on the edge of her thoughts, keeping her an-

chored—however fragilely—just this side of awareness.

Until the rumble of the tractor grew louder, pierc-
ing dreams and drawing her back into reality.

She sat up slowly and looked around. The light
dazzled her eyes. Shading them, she stared out over
the field.

A trail of dust rose behind the tractor. As she
watched, it came to a stop not far from where her car
sat. The motor was switched off. Mark opened the cab
door and climbed down.

He was dressed as she had seen him that first night,
in old jeans and a plaid work shirt. His hair was
mussed and once again he hadn't shaved. For several
moments he stood rubbing the back of his neck absently as he stared out over the neat furrows stretch-
ing across the vast field.

Only gradually did he realize that he wasn't alone.

Turning, he frowned through the sun's glare and
rising dust until he saw her.

"Lisa." His voice was soft, slightly rough as though
fatigue clung to it, but also with an unmistakably caressing quality that sent delicate tendrils of pleasure
down her back.

She got out of the car and walked toward the fence
without her eyes ever leaving him. The tractor was the
most modern kind, virtually a rolling truck with all the
comforts including air-conditioning. But the day was
too cool for that and he had left the windows open.

Fine particles of dust clung to his hair and to the
thick fringe of lashes around his eyes. He brushed
them away.

"How's the work going?" she asked, mostly because she couldn't think of anything else to say.

"Well enough." His eyes narrowed as they ran over her. He came closer and leaned against the fence. The sleeves of his shirt were rolled up to the elbows, exposing forearms browned by the sun and rippling with muscle. Quietly he said, "What's wrong?"

The question startled her. Surely he couldn't see into her mind? "Nothing," she insisted. "Why would anything be wrong?"

His broad shoulders rose and fell. "No reason, I just thought—" He broke off, looked at her steadily for a long moment, and without saying another word, ducked under the fence railing. The distance between them vanished.

Before she could move, his big hands closed gently but firmly on her shoulders. Holding her, he said, "Tell me what's happened."

It was uncanny, she thought, that he could do this. Here they were, standing on a winding country road amid the beauty of an early spring day, a man and a woman who by all rights barely knew each other.

And yet, in that sun-bright moment, she admitted deep inside that she had left her parents' home, the comfortable safety of her work, and come down this road seeking him. Knowing, in her heart, that she would find him in the bright, stirring day, find his strength and, it seemed, his wisdom.

And yet still, she wasn't quite ready to admit it all. Softly she said, "The superintendent of the building I lived in told me someone has been watching the place. He was concerned it might have something to do with Jimmy and me. But," she added hastily, "it probably doesn't matter anyway because we've left."

His hands tightened a fraction, just enough to make her wince. Instantly he eased his hold on her but didn't let go.

"You're telling me someone has been watching you?"

"Not me, the building where I used to live. There are over a hundred tenants. It might have nothing to do with me at all."

"But you don't deny the possibility. In fact, it's got you worried. Isn't that right?"

"Yes," she admitted, "but not very. I'm probably imagining things."

The look he shot her was pure exasperation. "Okay, that's it. Let's go."

"Where?" she demanded, even as she instinctively dug her heels in. Just what did he think he was doing?

"Over to the tractor. I've got a thermos of coffee and a pack of sandwiches. You're going to have some of each and tell me real slow what's going on."

The coffee actually sounded good, but she doubted the sandwiches would agree with her tension-tossed stomach. Ditto the idea of telling him about the fears that had driven her from New York. Pride made her reluctant to talk about her failed marriage and its lingering aftereffects.

"I have to get back to work," she said.

He looked at her as though she really had lost her mind. "Work? You're telling me someone may have been stalking you in New York and you expect to go back to *work?* Forget it. We're having this out right now."

Stalking. The word went straight through her. It was exactly the hard, brutal, terrifying truth she had been trying to avoid. What she'd run from hundreds of miles back to the only place where she could feel truly safe.

But safety was an illusion. If it existed at all, it lay only in her own strength and her fierce determination to protect her child at all costs.

They were back on the other side of the fence before she registered what had happened. Mark pushed her down gently on the tractor running board and reached inside the cab. He removed an insulated carry-all, uncorked the thermos and poured her a steaming cup.

"Here," he said gruffly, "drink this. You look white as a ghost."

She took a sip. It was bitterly strong coffee, just what she needed. She took a deep breath and in as few words as possible, told him what Fred Baker had said.

"It may mean nothing," she stressed. "Mr. Baker could be mistaken, although I admit it's a little hard to see how. But as I said, there are over a hundred tenants in the building. It's impossible to tell who the men are interested in."

"Baker's an ex-cop?" Mark asked. When she nodded, he said, "He's connected you to the surveillance without a whole lot of actual evidence. Is he the alarmist type?"

"On the contrary, he's as steady as they come."

"Then he's going with his gut, and if you've got any sense, you'll do the same. What led up to all this?"

"Led up?"

"Made you pack yourself, your boy and only a few belongings into your car and run like hell back here?"

Lisa took another sip of the coffee. It burned her tongue but she hardly felt it. She was battling pride, memory, the treacherous yearning to tell Mark all her troubles and somehow expect him to solve them balanced against the certain knowledge that she'd have to be a damn fool to ever trust a man so much again.

"You're exaggerating," she said. "I was a single parent living in the city. It's only natural that I'd take a chance on someplace better."

He got down on his haunches, the muscles of his thighs straining the worn fabric of his jeans, and looked her right in the eye. "You're lying."

Warm color stained her cheeks. "That's out of line."

"So's pretending you can handle everything on your own when you ought to know better. If someone's after you—even if it's only maybe—you owe it to yourself and to Jimmy to speak up about it." He leaned back slightly, giving her a little more room but not much. "Where's good old Chas these days?"

"I told you," she said, "he could be anywhere."

"New York?"

She started to shake her head but stopped. Any denial she might make stemmed only from what she hoped and prayed was true, not what she knew for sure.

"He never spent much time there," she said tentatively.

"And he never showed much interest in Jimmy. Right?"

Lisa turned her head away. Her throat was tight and she'd been wrong about the coffee, it had hit her stomach like molten lead.

"He helps to support him. The checks come through his lawyers. Look, if there *is* anything going on—and I'm not ready to say there is—it simply doesn't make any sense that Chas would be involved. He could have seen Jimmy anytime he wanted."

Her voice fell. Merely talking about the past forced her in a sense to relive it. She thought she'd put the pain to rest, but apparently she'd been wrong. It still hurt like hell.

"When Jimmy was born," she said softly, "I tried to convince Chas to be a part of his life to at least some degree. I would have gone along with just about any kind of visitation rights he could have wanted. But he simply wasn't interested. Why would he suddenly change and, not only that, but do it in such a bizarre way?"

"I don't know," Mark admitted. "But any man who would walk away from a woman who was carrying his child has to have something wrong with him to start with."

He fell silent, thinking over the situation. Lisa watched him. She thought he'd revealed more about himself than he knew with his last words. A bittersweet ache filled her.

She'd become so accustomed to taking care of herself and Jimmy that she no longer thought about what it would be like to have the support of a strong, loving man. Chas's checkbook conscience had made it easier to pay the monthly bills, although she'd accepted only an absolute minimum from him. It hadn't done anything for the sleepless nights, the worry, the hopes and the dreams that were all part of raising a child.

Abruptly Mark stood up. He held out a hand to her. Without thinking, she took it. "I'd like to talk to Baker myself," he said. Before she could answer, he went on.

"Hear me out before you say no. First, sometimes it helps to have another person's perspective on a situation. If I talk to him, maybe together we'd pick up something we're otherwise missing. Also, it can't hurt to let people know you aren't in this alone. Have you thought about what you're going to tell Chas's lawyers, the ones who send the checks?"

"I wasn't going to tell them anything," she said, "at least not until I have a better idea of what's going on."

He nodded approvingly. "Good. Now who knows where you went when you left the city?"

"Mr. Baker, several people I work with and the post office. That's it."

"Utility company? Bank? Friends? Neighbors?"

Lisa shook her head. "I left in a hurry."

"I got that impression." His voice softened. They were standing very close together. She could feel the heat of his body touching her own.

"How about it?" he said. "Would it really hurt to tell me why you left when you did?"

Lisa sighed. She'd come this far, she might as well go the rest of the way, even if it did make her sound foolish.

"There were crank calls, a breather. That's practically a sport in New York so maybe I shouldn't have thought anything of it. But at the same time that started happening, my baby-sitter said she thought someone was following her, and then I started to get the same feeling.''

"When you were out with Jimmy?"

She thought back, trying to recapture memories she had deliberately pushed aside. Slowly she said, "No, not just then. It happened several times when I was alone. I thought it was just nerves, but I couldn't be sure so finally I..."

"You did what you had to, Lisa," he said, and for just a moment the rough timbre of his voice made her think of bright water running over velvet-smooth stones.

"I thought I was overreacting," she said. The admission was hard, but the moment she said it, she felt better. She even managed to smile a little.

"Maybe you were," he acknowledged. "But you've got Jimmy to think of. Better safe, et cetera. And I meant it, I want to talk to Baker."

Lisa hesitated. She was completely unaccustomed to having anyone else handle her problems for her.

He saw her doubt and moved quickly to allay it. "I'll behave myself, I promise. I just want to hear for myself what he's got to say."

On the surface, it seemed a reasonable request. What was the big deal? He'd talk to the superintendent, hear that everything was under control, and that would be that.

Except that wasn't how it turned out.

Chapter 7

"I want you to move in here," Mark said.

They were standing in the great room of the main house, a vast, oak-beamed expanse of fieldstone and paneling that took up most of the first floor. He'd left Lisa there while he went to call Baker. The call had taken longer than she expected, more than half an hour. But now he was back—with a vengeance.

She stared at him in disbelief. Big as the room was, he seemed to fill it. She had a sudden sense of herself being just as easily dominated. Instinctively she rebelled against it.

"I won't do any such thing. I should never have involved you in the first place." Quickly she walked around him and headed for the door. "Now if you'll excuse me, I have to pick up Jimmy."

He didn't touch her. Not so much as a finger grazed her skin. But he did move, so quickly that she hardly saw it. Before she knew what was happening, he was standing directly in front of her, blocking her escape.

"Listen to me," he said. "Baker's a good guy. You're lucky he's there. Between when you talked to him and when I called, one of the men watching the building tried to tell the doorman that he was a friend of yours and that you wanted him to get something from your apartment. The doorman told him to get lost, but he was persistent. Baker had to go out himself and run him off. Even then, he only went as far as the car. He's still sitting there right in front of the building. He doesn't seem to care who sees him or what anyone thinks. Baker says it's going down quick."

"What does that mean?" Lisa asked. She could hardly think. One of the men had tried to get into her apartment. They really were after her. All the hopes she'd nurtured that none of it meant anything were gone, blown to smithereens by a handful of words.

"Coming to a head," Mark elaborated. "Getting dangerous. Now what haven't you told me?"

"Nothing!" The question shocked her. He'd already accused her once of lying. Was it going to become a habit?

He took a breath, visibly struggling to soften his approach. "I'm sorry, sometimes I forget this isn't the hockey rink. Look, I'm not trying to make things tougher for you, but there's definitely a problem here. Somebody is paying those men and paying them plenty. The only person you've mentioned with that kind of money is Chas. Why would he be doing this?"

Lisa shook her head in confusion. "I don't know. There is no reason. It's crazy."

Yet she couldn't ignore the possibility that it was also true. "I'm not sure what I believe about all this," she said. "But right now I have to go get Jimmy."

Deliberately she stepped around him and headed toward the door again. This time he let her go. Outside, he opened the door to her car for her and waited while she got in.

"Think about what I said," he told her.

She met his eyes for a moment, nodded once and turned the key in the ignition.

Mark watched the car drive away down the long road until it was out of sight. Only then did he go back inside the house. Beyond the great room was his office. He went straight there, shut the door, and picked up the phone.

In the slightly more than a year since he'd retired from hockey, he'd kept in touch with many of the players and coaches. But it wasn't them he thought of now.

Thumbing through his address file, he pulled out half a dozen names, all front-office men and in two cases actual owners. Men whose interest and contacts went far beyond the world of hockey and into the high finance sphere, where old money like Chas Howell's lived.

He had questions to ask and they were the men who just might be able to provide the answers.

Outside the bright spring sunshine faded as clouds moved across the sky. A splattering of rain fell against the windows.

By the time Lisa reached the house where Jimmy's play group met, it was raining hard. Jane's mother,

Nancy MacEnroe, opened the door for her. She was a tall, slender woman, like her daughter, with snow-white hair worn in a graceful bun and a ready smile that wreathed her hazel eyes in friendly wrinkles.

"Come on in," she said as she stepped aside for Lisa. "Isn't this some weather?"

Lisa pulled off the scarf she'd put on her head, tucked it into a pocket of her jacket and nodded. "Changeable, to say the least. How's everything?"

Nancy took the question as it was meant, less polite chitchat, more the honest concern of a mother whose child was in a new situation.

"Fine. Jimmy's a wonderful little boy. He's made several friends already and he seemed to have a good time."

Lisa smiled gratefully. She'd been worried about how Jimmy would react to being taken away from the friends he'd known in the city, but it seemed now that there'd been no reason for concern. Her son had a steady, cheerful nature that helped him take new situations in stride.

"He especially liked the sandbox," Nancy added as she led Lisa toward the big playroom at the back of the house. The rain had driven the children inside, but they didn't seem to mind. Two girls and a boy, all about Jimmy's age, were busy building a castle out of blocks.

"Now where did he go to?" Nancy murmured. She bent down to look in a cardboard puppet theater. With a shake of her head, she said, "Maybe he's in the bathroom."

But the small room off the main play area was empty. Nor was Jimmy hiding in the supply closet or in the Indian tepee.

Lisa's heart began to beat just a little faster. She told herself not to be silly. Nancy MacEnroe was a caring and trustworthy person. She had known Jane's mother all her life and had, as a child herself, played many times under Nancy's watchful eye.

Running a day-care center as she did, she was even more safety conscious than ever. There were child guards on all the windows and doors. Jimmy couldn't possibly have left the house by himself.

But then where was he?

"The kitchen," Nancy said. "I'll bet he's getting some more of those peanut butter crackers he liked."

Lisa nodded. That had to be it. Jimmy was a self-reliant child used to getting things for himself. He'd be in the kitchen, probably smeared with peanut butter.

When she scooped him up, he'd get it all over her, but she wouldn't mind. She just wanted the reassurance of holding him, of knowing that he was all right...

The kitchen was empty.

"Where is he?" Her voice sounded harsh even to her own ears.

Nancy frowned. "I don't understand. He has to be here somewhere. The children can't open the doors by themselves."

"I know," Lisa said quickly. "I saw. Are there any other adults here?"

"Just me. Let's check the play area again."

But when they did, there was still no sign of Jimmy.

Lisa's stomach was clenched into a hard, aching knot. She knew she had to stay calm, the worst thing she could do would be to panic. But her heart was beating even faster and a horrible sense of dread threatened to swallow her up.

"Easy," Nancy said when she saw the look on her face. "Four-year-olds get curious. Maybe he decided to explore."

Lisa gave a short, quick nod. "I'll take a look in the basement."

"I'll do the same upstairs," Nancy said.

They separated. The basement door also had a child protector on the knob, the kind that was supposed to make it impossible for anyone other than an adult to open. It had to be squeezed from all directions at once in order to release the latch.

Jimmy couldn't possibly have done that, but Lisa decided to check, anyway. A bare light bulb hung over the stairs. She flicked it on and took a quick look around.

Nancy's basement was neat and tidy. There was the usual furnace and hot water tank, along with several old bicycles and a cluster of boxes stacked against one wall. Lisa was just moving the boxes to look behind them when she heard Nancy call to her.

She took the steps two at a time. Nancy was waiting, one arm around a sheepish-looking Jimmy.

"A few nights ago when I was baby-sitting I told him how you and Jane liked to climb into the window seat in her room and watch the birds in the tree outside. He decided to give it a try."

Lisa all but sagged with relief. She got down on her knees in front of Jimmy. Softly she said, "We didn't know where you'd gone to."

"I'm sorry, Mommy," he murmured. "I know I'm not supposed to go anywhere without telling you, but I just wanted to see."

He looked so genuinely contrite that Lisa's smile wobbled. She reached out a gentle hand to brush aside the lock of hair that had fallen into his eyes. The last thing she wanted was for her own fears to affect Jimmy. He deserved a normal, happy life.

"It's okay," she assured him. "No harm done. Now what do you say we go home, buddy? I've got a plate of chocolate-chip cookies that could use some attention."

He cheered up instantly and raced off to say goodbye to the other children. While they waited for him, Nancy asked quietly, "Everything all right now?"

Lisa's nod was rueful. "I'm sorry if I seem like an alarmist."

"Don't apologize. You've been through an upheaval. It's only natural to feel a little tense." She paused a moment. "There's nothing else to it, is there?"

Slowly Lisa said, "There may be a problem with my ex-husband." Saying the words out loud gave shape and form to her fear. She couldn't deny it any longer.

Something was going terribly wrong in her life and it could end up threatening Jimmy. No matter what, she had to protect him.

Nancy touched her arm gently. "Maybe you ought to have a word with the sheriff. If you've got any concerns about your safety or Jimmy's, he should know."

"I just may do that."

Jimmy came bouncing back. He threw himself into her arms. She laughed, holding him close, and carried him out to the car.

But even as she made sure he was buckled in, and waved to Nancy, she was thinking about what she'd be able to tell the sheriff.

That a man back in New York said her apartment was being watched. That there'd been some phone calls. That she was very afraid.

It didn't add up to much. When she forced herself to think about it coldly and logically, she had to wonder why it was enough to spark the stomach-clenching anxiety that seemed to be growing inside her with each passing moment.

Her hands tightened on the steering wheel. Rain slashed against the windshield. The wipers flicked back and forth at top speed but they couldn't do anything about the tears that blurred her vision.

She blinked fiercely, refusing to cry. She'd shed enough tears in the past. Now she had to be strong. Nancy and Jane meant well, and her parents certainly loved her, but in the final analysis she couldn't depend on anyone except herself.

And Mark.

She shook her head impatiently. She'd gotten into this fix by trusting a man. No way was she dumb enough to think she could get out the same way.

Besides, she barely knew him. Never mind that he seemed to have a direct pipeline into her hormones, the fact was that the man was practically a stranger.

She was on her own and the worst mistake she could make would be to pretend otherwise.

Through everything that had happened between her and Chas, she had never become vindictive. Angry, yes, and certainly hurt. But never once had she given in to the urge to wish him ill.

Until now.

If he came near Jimmy, if he threatened him in any way, she would do anything she had to in order to stop him.

Anything at all.

Chapter 8

The phone was ringing. Lisa could hear it as she got out of the car. Juggling a bag of groceries and her purse, she opened the back door quickly and reached for the receiver.

"Hello?"

It was several days after her conversation with Fred Baker, the meeting with Mark and the scare at Nancy's house. Since then nothing out of the ordinary had happened.

Mark had called several times to make sure everything was all right, but when she assured him that it was, he seemed satisfied. Jimmy continued to go to the play group and was thriving. Lisa was getting a fair amount of work done and was feeling better about life in general.

"Hello?"

Silence. She could hear static over the line but otherwise there was nothing. Her mouth tightened. She dropped the receiver back into its cradle as though it had burned her.

Her hands were trembling as she set the grocery bags down on the counter. Automatically she began putting her purchases away in the cabinets and refrigerator.

When she caught herself trying to fit the breakfast cereal into the freezer, she stopped and took a deep breath.

She was not going to let this throw her. People got crank calls all the time. They meant nothing.

Besides, she had no reason to think there'd even been anyone on the other end. She hadn't even heard any breathing.

But then she hadn't in New York, either.

It didn't matter. She was home, Jimmy was safe, everything was going to be fine.

She put the cereal where it belonged and folded the now empty bags. When that was done, she took a quick look around and decided the house could survive another day without being vacuumed. She was just switching on her computer when the phone rang again.

Lisa hesitated. On the fourth ring, the answering machine would pick up. But before that could happen, her curiosity got the better of her. She lifted the receiver and put it to her ear gingerly.

"Hello?"

"Ms. Morley?" Fred Baker's voice boomed over the line. "I've got some good news for you, I think. Those men haven't shown up today."

Relief flowed through her. She sat back more comfortably in her chair. "That does sound good," she said. A tiny flicker of worry curled around the edges of her mind. "Doesn't it?"

"I'm hoping it means they've been called off. Whoever's been paying them must have decided there wasn't any point continuing. How's everything there?"

"Fine," she said quickly. "No problems." She wasn't going to mention the phone call that had probably been nothing more than a crossed wire.

"Good, glad to hear it. By the way, I sure got a surprise when Mark Fletcher called. I was a big fan of his." He chuckled. "He was tough as nails on the ice. Nothing got past him. Didn't sound like he's changed much."

"I guess not," Lisa said. Grateful as she was to Mark for his help, she didn't want to discuss him. She had done her best in the past few days not to even think about him. Not with any great success, of course, but she had tried.

"Mr. Baker," she asked quietly, "is there any reason to think the men may not have been called off?"

The superintendent hesitated. She waited through the space of several seconds before he said, "Only one reason I can think of, that's if they realize there's no point keeping watch here because you're gone."

"Could they know that?"

"They've got to at least suspect it. After days of watching without a single sighting of you, it must have occurred to them that you'd flown the coop. Question is, are they going to be able to figure out where you've gone?"

"I don't know," Lisa said softly. "I guess that depends on who they are, or more important, who was paying them."

"That ex-husband of yours, he knows about Langston?"

"He heard me talk about it, but we never actually got out here together. It's possible he wouldn't even remember."

Silence again as Fred Baker thought things over. Quietly he asked, "Were you born there?"

"No," she said, a little puzzled as to why he would ask. "My parents were living down in Florida then. They moved here when I was two years old."

"That's good. And you were living in New York when you got married. So your license application says Florida for your place of birth and New York for your residence. There's nothing on it about Langston."

"No," Lisa agreed. The implications began to sink in. Any stranger—even a trained investigator—looking into her background would not have an easy time discovering Langston. Her marriage license, divorce papers, employment record, all listed Florida and New York.

Before meeting Chas, she hadn't been in the city long enough to really make friends. And afterward, with everything that happened, she hadn't had the time or inclination to confide in people.

Without even realizing it, she had left a trail that would be difficult to follow. Except by someone who really knew her.

A short time later, after she had hung up the phone, she sat very still in the chair behind her desk and tried to convince herself that the danger, whatever it had been, was over.

She couldn't manage it. Her eyes drifted again to the phone. She had to resist the urge to call Nancy to be sure everything was all right with Jimmy.

Finally she turned her attention to work. It was just difficult and absorbing enough to distract her. She took a short break for lunch but otherwise worked straight through until it was time to pick up Jimmy.

Driving to get him, she forced herself to stay slightly below the speed limit. When she reached Nancy's house, she parked and got out. Even before she came around to the back, she heard the happy shouts of children.

Jimmy was in the sandbox. His hair was tousled, his eyes bright with laughter and his cheeks flushed with healthy color.

Watching him, an upsurge of love struck her that was so powerful it momentarily robbed her of breath. Not all the riches in the world could have equaled the sight of her child, happy and safe.

She called to him and he jumped up, running full tilt into her arms so that she laughed and swung him up, making him squeal in delight. "Come see what I did," he demanded.

She set him down and went hand-in-hand to inspect the hillocks of sand, the carefully made tunnels, the towers festooned with sticks.

"Terrific," she said, and hugged him, feeling the solid beat of his heart close beneath her own.

Mark sat in his pickup truck in front of Lisa's house. He figured he'd missed her by just a few minutes but he was satisfied to wait. If he read the situation right, she'd come straight back with Jimmy.

Although he hadn't spoken with her in several days, he had run into Jane MacEnroe the previous afternoon. She'd given him a long level look, asked how he was doing and mentioned that Lisa seemed to be sticking pretty close to home.

He hadn't even pretended to wonder why she was telling him that. Although he didn't know Jane well, he did know that she cared about Lisa.

"I'll be going by there tomorrow," he'd said, and left it at that.

So here he was, parked in front of her door, with the radio on low and a song about lost love strumming softly in the background. If anyone had asked him, he wouldn't have been able to say exactly why he was doing this.

Logically he should have been back in his office where the usual three dozen things waited to be taken care of. Instead he sat, fingers tapping lightly on the steering wheel, and gazed at the Morley house.

He remembered it well. It was one of those houses he'd driven by occasionally when he was in high school, just to remind himself that they existed. Houses with neat lawns, curtains at the windows, flowers out in front, bright lights on when evening came. Houses for people like Lisa.

His smile was rueful. The old pain wasn't completely gone, but it was only a faint remnant of what it had been. He'd left the past behind when he cut loose from Langston, heading for the bright lights, the quicksilver flash of ice and the deafening roar of victory.

He'd come back a different man, exactly as he'd intended to. Sure, he wished he'd had a better childhood, but he'd gotten through it and he'd moved on. It was now that counted.

And yet, looking at Lisa's house, he still felt a little twinge of longing deep down inside. His own house was far larger and grander, but it lacked a certain something, the spark that turned four walls and a roof into a home. He sighed and closed his eyes for a moment. Introspection wasn't his strong point. He didn't precisely avoid it, but neither did he seek it out.

He was there because it was the right thing to do, plain and simple. Lisa was a woman alone with a child. He was a neighbor and a friend. He had a responsibility to help.

The fact that she filled him with a tantalizing mixture of hard-driving need and melting tenderness was a complication he'd just as soon not deal with right now.

He cracked an eye open, glanced in the rearview mirror and saw her car approaching. Slowly he unfolded his long body and got out. By the time she pulled into the driveway, he was leaning against the big oak tree nearby, hands pushed deeply into the pockets of his jeans and a slight smile lifting the corners of his chiseled mouth.

She looked good. A little tired, to be sure, and surprised to see him, but good all the same. Her feathery auburn hair curled slightly along the slender column of her throat. She wasn't wearing any makeup, her cheeks were slightly flushed and her mouth was softly ripe. A plain white shirt with rolled-up sleeves was tucked into jeans that clung to her firm bottom. He made a deliberate effort to stop staring, and pushed himself away from the tree.

"Afternoon," he said, and turned his attention to Jimmy.

Before he caught sight of Mark, the boy had been bouncing around exuberantly and talking a mile a minute. But now he stood quiet and watchful beside his mother, never taking his eyes from Mark's face.

Slowly Mark bent down so that they were looking at each other directly. "You're Jimmy," he said.

The boy nodded but did not smile. "Who are you?"

"Mark Fletcher. I live near here. Your mom and I used to go to school together."

That piqued Jimmy's curiosity. As most four-year-olds, he thought his mother had always been exactly as she was now. The idea of her going to school was novel enough to distract him.

"Like my school?" he asked.

Mark grinned, pretending to be surprised. "Don't tell me you're in school already?"

"Nursery school," Jimmy admitted with a modest shrug. He looked at Mark again. His eyes were hazel, filled with the same green and gold glints as Lisa's.

But his features were different, stronger and broader, the nose another shape altogether, the brows straight instead of slanting and the mouth slightly thinner. His father's features.

A spurt of anger went through Mark. Anger at the unknown man who had left such a son to grow up without him. And hard on it, compassion for the boy who faced him so steadily, all the while standing close beside his mother as though to both draw strength from her and return it as best he could.

Mark stood up. He put a hand lightly on Jimmy's shoulder. Looking at Lisa, he said, "I thought you two might like to go out to dinner."

Chapter 9

"This is outright bribery," Lisa said. She stood with her hands on her hips, turning her head first in one direction and then the other as she took in the whole incredible scene. She'd never seen anything like it in her life.

The entire field at the far end of Mark's property was occupied by the carny people. They'd come in the night with their trailers and trucks, and were busy setting up shop. For the next three days, Langston would be entertained by the World-Famous Bingham & Hardestry Traveling Carnival, Toast of Seven Continents.

Signs advertising the show had been up around town since before she arrived. She'd noticed them and had made a mental note to take Jimmy once the carny opened. Never in her wildest dreams could she have imagined that he would receive his very own, very exclusive preview.

"Bribery," she repeated as she tore her eyes away and turned back to Mark. "Plain and simple."

He sighed in mock contrition. "It's true. I asked myself what a four-year-old boy would like. Wouldn't you know it, the answer that popped into my head was his very own carnival."

"Which you just happened to have right here in your very own field?"

"Timing is everything in life."

She laughed. They were sitting on the ground beside his pickup, on a blanket he had thoughtfully provided. It was getting on for sundown. Strings of yellow lights illuminated the field where the carny people were working.

The Bingham carnival was one of the few left in the country still under canvas. Already the main tent had been hoisted into place with several smaller ones set up nearby.

They'd had dinner in one of those, sharing it with the teams of roustabouts and the carny acts. The food had been surprisingly good—hearty stew and fresh-baked bread, apple cobbler and tangy lemonade.

Jimmy had been almost too excited to eat. Lisa shook her head wryly as she remembered his huge-eyed, head-swiveling fascination. Finally he'd gotten enough down to satisfy her. She'd let him watch as the rest of the equipment was set up, so long as he didn't get under foot and stayed where she could see him.

He was doing that now, bouncing from one foot to the other as roustabouts worked to set up the carousel. In the swaying yellow lights, the painted horses almost looked alive.

Memory flowed through her. Softly she said, "The carny's been coming here a long time."

Mark nodded. "Long as I can remember. One of the few things Ben Harris asked me for when he sold out was that I go on letting them use this field."

"I'm glad you did. The world changes so fast, it's nice to see a little bit of the past stay the same."

"When the carny was in town, I practically lived at it."

"Me, too," Lisa said. "The only time I ever cut school was to come here."

He pretended to be shocked. "Cut? Lisa Morley? There goes the last of my illusions."

"Hey, listen, I wasn't such a goody-goody. I did some things."

"Oh, yeah, what did you do?" he teased. "Hide the erasers? Let somebody copy your homework?"

"Is that what you really thought of me? A total weenie?"

"No," he said softly. "I thought you were an incredibly beautiful girl from a world I could hardly imagine."

Lisa's breath caught. He spoke so simply, yet the passion and truth of his words was unmistakable. All that time when she'd been thinking of him—half drawn to, half afraid of the wildness he seemed to embody—he had been gazing at her across the gulf that separated them with a yearning she had never suspected but could no longer ignore.

A soft sigh escaped her. She gazed out over the carny tents, watching her son staring with rapt fascination as magic sprang up before him, and felt deep within the all-but-forgotten longings of her own childhood, the wish for something good, true and imperishable.

Had anyone asked her just a short time ago, she would have scoffed at the notion that she was still capable of such dreams. What hopes she had were wrapped up in Jimmy. Or so she had thought. Now she had to reconsider.

The soft evening air wrapped around them. In the glow of the carny lights and the fading sun, the billowing tents seemed cloudlike, as though floating above the ordinary world.

She sighed again and moved, ever so slightly, her hand reaching tentatively across inches, across miles, across years, to gently brush Mark's fingers.

He turned his head, saying nothing, no sound disturbing the sudden stillness wrapping around them. Or perhaps there were noises, in the distance from the carny, and she didn't hear them because of the blood, rushing, dancing, surging, through her, carrying the hot, sweet languor of anticipation.

His head bent, dark against the gathering night. She waited, heart beating, alive, waiting . . . suddenly no longer as fearful as she had been for the past was sliding away, down the long avenues of the carny lit by strings of colored bulbs, away into shadowed memory, fading fast.

Until there was only now, this moment, alone among the scent of hay bales and canvas, campfires and night air. Alone—

His mouth was hard, without the gentleness she remembered from before. A man's mouth, demanding, taking, yet also so sweetly giving that her breath caught in her throat.

Then she was in his arms, strong bands around her, drawing strength from him, drawing solace and giving, too, as the passion there from the first instant caught flame within them both.

His tongue thrust slowly, penetrating her. She gasped, shocked by pleasure so acute it teetered on the edge of pain. A kiss, she thought in the far distant regions of her mind where thought was still possible. Nothing more, only a kiss.

And yet when had she felt like this, truly? When had she been so taken out of herself, made one with the night and the fire and the stars whirling overhead?

Trembling, they moved apart and gazed at each other, stunned, questioning, uncertain.

"Lisa . . ." he said, his voice low and rough, caressing her. "I—"

"Mommy, Mommy! Look at me!" Jimmy yelled above the calliope music. He was astride a proud black steed, hands clutching the silver pole, riding up and down, around and around, the sole passenger on the premier ride of the carousel.

Lisa took a deep, shuddering breath. She didn't know whether to be relieved by her son's interruption or to regret it. Her hand shook as she raised it to wave.

Jimmy waved back, his small face alight with joy. She couldn't recall ever having seen him quite so happy.

Mark was beside her, close but not touching. She was vividly aware of his size and strength, the quiet certainty deep within him, and the gentleness that had made him give a fatherless four-year-old boy this gift he would never forget.

Quietly she said, "Thank you."

He turned slightly so that their eyes met. "For what?"

She made a gesture, a little awkwardly for she was suddenly very nervous. "For this, all of it. For Jimmy."

Her throat was tight. She could feel her mouth beginning to tremble and pressed her lips close together. Emotions she didn't want to confront were painfully close to the surface.

Mark shot her a look that suggested he saw and understood everything without any need for words. "He's a good kid."

"Yes, he is." There was an undercurrent of anger in her words. Jimmy was a good kid, a bright and loving boy. He hadn't asked to be fathered by a man who didn't feel up to the task. But he was paying the price for it no matter how hard she tried to protect him.

Tears burned her eyes. Taken unaware by the sudden fierce sweep of feeling that tore through her, she turned away hastily.

Mark's hand was gentle on her shoulder. He stood close behind her so that she could feel the broad span of his chest against her back. The temptation to lean against him almost overwhelmed her.

"It's okay," he said. "You're allowed to be human."

"Is that what this is?" she asked, and managed a shaky laugh. "I feel more like something that's gone through the wringer."

"Like I said, human. You're a good mother."

A small spurt of pleasure coiled inside her. "I try. Hardly a day goes by that I don't wonder if I'm doing something wrong, but I understand that's part of the job."

"Lisa..."

She looked at him over her shoulder, too quickly for she hadn't fully realized exactly how close they were. His breath touched her cheek.

"What is it?" she murmured.

He tore his eyes from her and looked toward Jimmy, who was still fully occupied with the carousel. "I made some calls."

"Who to?"

"People. I wanted to know more about Chas."

She stiffened. "Why didn't you just ask me?"

"Because I didn't want to upset you. I'd have to be deaf, dumb and blind not to know that you don't like to talk about the guy, and who could blame you? Besides, I figured there might be one or two things you didn't know."

Lisa stared at him incredulously. She still couldn't believe he had violated her privacy without a qualm. "Like what?"

"Where he is these days, for instance. What he's doing." Seeing the look on her face, he went on hastily, "Look, get mad if you want, but we both know he's the first person you think of when you try to figure out what's going on. If it turned out he really was helicopter skiing in Outer Mongolia or whatever, you'd write him off. But as it happens, good old Chas came back to the States a couple of weeks ago."

"How do you know that?" Lisa demanded. Shock piled on shock. Chas was back? He wasn't thousands

of miles away doing who knew what? He was where?
How close? Doing what?

"Somebody I know, a team owner, happened to run
into him at some political fund-raiser."

"Chas doesn't go to that kind of thing."

"Well, he did a week ago Thursday."

She shook her head stubbornly. "Your friend's
wrong. He hates anything like that."

"Then he's changed," Mark insisted. "They had a
drink together and talked about climbing K-2 in the
Himalayas. Ring a bell?"

Lisa felt a sinking sensation deep within. Faintly she
said, "Chas climbed that mountain several years ago."
More strongly she added, "But just because he happens to be in the country doesn't mean he has anything to do with what's been going on."

Mark shook his head. He was clearly working hard
at patience. "It's only natural that you would defend
him but—"

"Natural?" she interrupted. "Why on earth would
I defend him? We're talking about the bum who
walked out on me when I was pregnant and who's
never bothered to spend even five minutes with his
son, aren't we? Natural? It would be *natural* for me to
shove him into the nearest deep hole and roll a boul-
der over it. *That's* natural."

Her cheeks flushed, she glared at Mark. "Let's get
something straight right now. I am not carrying a
torch, or anything else, for Chas. Whatever I felt for
him—and I'm not sure what that was—I got over it a
long time ago. If he's got anything to do with what's
been going on, I'll feed his liver to the birds for
breakfast. Got that?"

Mark took a quick step back and held up his hands. He was grinning broadly and his eyes, when they touched her, made her feel very warm.

"Got it."

"What are you smiling at?"

"Nothing. I wouldn't dare."

"Liar. What's so funny?"

"Little Lisa Morley grew up."

She looked him right in the eye, sinking into blue brilliant as the heavens at noon, tumbling over dreams that had stayed with her through all the years, all the upsets and all the disappointments.

The music of the calliope swirled around them. Mark suddenly grabbed her hand. He moved so quickly she had no chance to protest.

His arm was steel around her waist, his laughter sure and irresistible. She was lifted, high, higher, onto the back of a prancing golden horse.

"Carousels aren't only for children," he murmured, and with a single, smooth movement mounted beside her.

Jimmy looked back over his shoulder, delighted by the grown-ups joining in his play. "It's fun, Mommy!"

And it was, there on the carousel, going around and around, caught within the music and the moment with no thought for anything beyond the fragile realm of dreams.

Chapter 10

The ringing phone woke Lisa. She picked it up groggily, automatically. It was raining again, a wet, cold morning when any sensible—and fortunate—soul snuggled down under the covers without compunction.

"'Lo?"

Silence.

Lisa's eyes had crept shut again. Now they opened wide and stayed that way.

"Hello? Who is this?"

Nothing, only static and this time, unmistakably, the sense that there was someone—a presence, a feeling—on the other end.

Who is this?

Lisa sat up straighter. Her heart was beating very fast. "Chas, if this is you, listen to me. If you do any-thing—*anything*—to harm Jimmy, I swear you'll wish

you had never been born. I offered you every chance
to be with him. I pleaded with you, for God's sake!
You walked straight out of our lives. Stay that way!
Do you hear me? Chas? *Chas?*"

Click.

Whoever was on the other end had hung up. Lisa
put the phone down slowly. She was trembling all over.
Bile rose in the back of her throat. A hand over her
mouth, she jumped out of bed and ran for the bathroom.

Twenty minutes later she was in the kitchen, wan
but functioning. Jimmy was still asleep. She was
grateful for that but not for a whole lot more.

While the coffee brewed, she went into the living
room at the front of the house and looked through the
windows. Except for the parked cars of her neighbors, the street was empty. No one was watching her
house, at least not yet.

Jimmy woke a short time later. She got his breakfast and laid out his clothes, all the while trying not to
fuss over him too much. He was happy, chattering on
about the wonderful time he'd had at the carny, and
looking forward to getting to Nancy's.

She drove him there shortly before nine o'clock. The
weather seemed to be trying to clear. Rays of sunlight
broke through the clouds just as she pulled up at the
house. Trying to see that as a good omen, she got out
and walked up the flagstone path.

Jimmy raced ahead, anxious to be with the other
children. Lisa followed more slowly. She spoke briefly
with Nancy, handed over Jimmy's lunch and then
forced herself to leave.

Getting back into her car, she sat behind the wheel for several minutes, staring at the house. Finally she realized that she had to drive away. Part of protecting Jimmy meant keeping him from the fear that was fast becoming her constant companion.

She went down the street and turned left in the direction of her own house. Doubt assailed her. She couldn't simply go home and get to work. In her present state there was no possibility of her being able to concentrate.

But neither did she want to drive around aimlessly. Her foot eased on the accelerator. She hesitated, trying to decide what to do.

It was shortly after nine. Jane would be at work, and besides, Lisa didn't want to bother her. She could call Mark. The thought came of its own accord, as natural as the breath that filled her lungs, unbidden, life-giving, instinctive.

She could call Mark.

So simple, so tempting. He was a strong, confident, giving man. He could take care of everything. She could stop worrying, stop fighting, stop struggling. It would be so easy.

Too easy. The temptation to turn to him was so great that it frightened her. It seemed to signal a kind of surrender that she couldn't accept. To do so, she would have to be able to trust, and that was simply beyond her.

No, she wouldn't call Mark. She would do what she probably should have done her first day back. Relieved simply at having made a decision, she put her foot down more firmly on the accelerator and turned right at the corner, heading into town.

* * *

The sheriff's office was next to the town hall in a small, red brick building that had replaced a much older wooden structure. The front, immediately beyond the entrance, was taken up by a seating area, a counter and behind that the chairs and desks of the deputies.

Sheriff Bill Nagel had an office in the back, across the hall from the two small holding cells. The deputy escorted her there, asked if she wanted a cup of coffee, and when told no, left. Bill Nagel came in a few minutes later.

He was a short, sandy-haired man with a muscular build and a military bearing. In his early forties, he'd been born and bred in Langston.

People said part of what made him so good at his job was that he knew most every secret that had ever existed in the town and that those he didn't know weren't worth the trouble. For all that, he had a relaxed and friendly air about him that concealed a sharp mind and strong conscience.

Lisa did not know him well. She'd been gone from the town for all the years he'd been sheriff, but she did remember him vaguely from her childhood, when he'd been a deputy sent around to the school to tell the kids to live right.

Naturally they'd all wanted to touch his gun. He'd brought a teddy bear along that he let them play with instead.

Funny, she thought as she met his steady gaze, the things a person would remember.

Nagel smiled slightly and held out his hand. "Morning, Miss Morley."

He didn't fumble her name, as though trying to remember what her husband had been called or questioning why she'd dropped his surname. She was Lisa Morley to him, citizen of Langston, and deserving of his straightforward attention.

"What can I do for you?" he asked after they had shaken hands. He took his place in the chair behind the desk and continued to look at her directly.

His scrutiny was like the rest of him—frank, open and unprejudiced. Whatever he'd heard about her coming back, he hadn't jumped to any conclusions.

Lisa took a deep breath. Her hands were clasped in her lap. She felt better now that the sheriff was actually there but she still had doubts.

"I'm not sure I should be here," she said quietly.

Nagel leaned back in his chair, stretched his legs out and nodded. "Okay. Suppose we just chat awhile? How's your boy doing?"

"Jimmy's fine," she said with a faint smile. "He goes to Mrs. MacEnroe for day care."

"She's a good woman. You settling in all right?"

"Pretty much. I do freelance programming—maybe you've heard that—and I'm lucky to have plenty of work. In fact, it's easier to do it here than in New York. There are fewer distractions."

She paused, feeling the half-truth of what she'd just said. Quietly she added, "At least there ought to be. The fact is—"

"Go on," Nagel said gently. He wasn't rushing her, just letting her know that he was there to listen.

"I'm not sure," she said slowly, "but I think I may have a problem with my ex-husband."

"Jimmy's father?"

"That's right. Before we left New York, I was getting crank calls and it seemed that someone was following us. The superintendent of the building where we lived tells me that a team of men was watching the place for several days after we left and that one of them claimed to be a friend of mine."

"Any chance of it being true? I mean, could somebody you worked with have gotten alarmed when you left and tried to check things out?"

"No," Lisa said, shaking her head. "I had finished the job I'd been working on and I was just about to start the one I'm doing now. There was no reason for anyone to be alarmed, much less to send people to watch where I lived."

"Okay," Nagel said. He picked up a pencil on the desk and turned it around between his fingers thoughtfully. "Anything since you got here?"

"Phone calls. At first I told myself it was just a coincidence, but it happened again this morning. Somebody calls and doesn't say anything."

"Somebody? You mean your ex-husband?"

"I don't know," Lisa admitted. She clasped her hands more tightly. They were starting to shake. "But I have found out that Chas is back in this country. That's unusual for him. He spends most of his time traveling."

"How did you find that out?"

She hesitated, but having come this far, it didn't make much sense to back down now. "Mark Fletcher heard it from someone he knows. He's aware of what's been happening and he seems to think there may be some reason for concern."

"I see . . ." the sheriff said slowly. He straightened up in the chair, discarding the pencil. His gaze focused on the wall over her shoulder. She could almost hear his mind turning over what she'd told him.

Finally he said, "I might as well be straight with you, Miss Morley. Mark called me yesterday. He didn't tell me the details you've provided, but he did say he thought maybe I ought to be keeping a closer watch on your place."

Lisa was startled. She hadn't considered that Mark would do any such thing. "That was very forward of him. This is my problem, after all."

Nagel looked amused. "Sure it is," he said soothingly. "But there's no harm getting a little help, is there? That's why you're here. Anyway, we did a drive by twice last night and didn't see anything."

"Oh . . ." Lisa said, feeling flustered. She'd slept through the night, unaware that the sheriff's office was keeping watch over her. Now she didn't know whether to feel foolish or grateful, or both.

"It's my job," Nagel said. He seemed to sense her unease. "Besides, I know I'd answer to Fletcher if I didn't and I'd just as soon not do that."

He was smiling as he spoke but the words were serious. He meant what he said.

"I didn't realize you and Mark knew each other that well."

His smile deepened. "Heck, he was my first arrest. I was a newly minted deputy and he was a hell-bent-for-leather kid. I remember it like it was yesterday."

Lisa opened her mouth and then shut it again. She had absolutely no idea what she was supposed to say to such a revelation. "That's nice," definitely didn't fit.

Nagel seemed to be enjoying himself. He had a nostalgic gleam in his eye.

"I gave him the usual lecture about heading down a slippery path. He gave me the usual go-to-hell answer. We had a few more go-rounds after that, but don't you know it, every single year he was in the championships, he sent me tickets? And didn't I go? Hell, he was the best I ever saw on ice. You ask anybody, they'll tell you he brought something special to the game."

"Were you surprised when he retired?" Lisa asked.

It was definitely off the subject, but she couldn't resist. The temptation to know more about Mark wouldn't be ignored.

"Surprised? No, I couldn't say I was that, although it was a tremendous loss. But he'd had a fantastic career and he went out on top. You can't ask for better than that."

"No, I guess you can't. What about when he decided to come back here?"

"That was no surprise. He'd been talking about it for years. Every time we saw each other, he'd ask me about places up for sale. I think it was Ben Harris deciding to retire that maybe made Mark figure his time had come, too. Anyway, the point of all this is that I take what he says real seriously. If you don't mind a little advice, I think you ought to do the same. Maybe there's nothing to this business with the phone calls, but the stuff back in New York sure doesn't sound good."

Nagel leaned back in his chair again, folded his hands behind his head, and appeared to settle in for a long stretch.

"Now suppose you tell me all about this ex-husband of yours and just what it is you think he might be up to."

Slowly, choosing her words with great care, Lisa did as he asked.

Chapter 11

Lisa felt better after she left the sheriff's office. At least she'd done something about the situation. Nagel hadn't been able to offer a whole lot of help, but he did assure her that he and his men would keep a close eye on the house.

He also suggested that she try getting in touch with Chas directly and tell him that she'd gone to the police. Whether he was actually involved or not, it couldn't hurt.

She was still thinking about how to go about that if she decided she wanted to when she reached the house. She left the car in the driveway, went inside, and put on a fresh pot of coffee.

There were still five hours left before she was due to pick up Jimmy. With luck, she'd get some real work done.

When the coffee was ready, she poured a cup and took it into her office. She was just settling down when the phone rang.

Her hand jumped. A line of *K's* appeared across the screen. Muttering under her breath, she reached for the phone.

"Hello?"

Silence.

Lisa's mouth tightened. This time she'd been caught wide awake and with a shot of confidence from her talk with Nagel.

The urge to let loose was strong but she controlled it. Remembering the first rule for dealing with nuisance callers, she took a deep breath, let half of it go, and with great precision, hung up the phone.

That done, she took a sip of the coffee, pressed the delete button to get rid of the row of *K's,* and started back to work.

The phone rang.

Lisa stopped typing and stared at it. It could be Nancy, or Jane, or Mark, or Nagel, or somebody selling magazine subscriptions. It could be a wrong number.

"Hello?"

Silence.

Anger rose in her. All those words she knew perfectly well but didn't normally use clambered to be let out, just this once. Instead she thought of what Nagel had said about getting in touch with Chas and decided that just maybe she'd been saved the trouble.

"I've gone to the police," she said slowly and clearly. "The sheriff knows about what's going on and about New York. There are patrol cars watching the house.''

And then for good measure—and because she was truly feeling desperate—she added, ''I think you should also know that I have a gun. I was taught to use it as a child and I'm still a good shot. Don't make the mistake of thinking that I'll hesitate for even a second.''

Silence still, but the faint breathing she could hear was definitely quicker than before.

''I'm going to hang up again. I'll also be leaving the answering machine on, so there's not much point in you continuing to do this. Remember, the police know about you, but I'm not just counting on them. I'm armed and I'll do anything I have to.''

The words seemed to echo in the quiet of the room as she hung up the phone. She sat, staring at it. An icy calmness had settled over her.

But it wasn't enough to protect her from the implications of what she had said. She had issued a challenge, one she'd better be prepared to live up to.

Under the circumstances, there was no sense trying to work. She left the computer on and went upstairs. The metal box was in the back of the closet, right where it had always been. So was the key in the dresser.

She set the box on the bed and unlocked it. The hinges squeaked slightly as she lifted the lid. Inside was her father's .35.

At one time he'd also had several rifles, but he'd gotten rid of those when he gave up hunting. The .35 he'd kept partly out of sentiment and partly because he still liked to target shoot.

It was the gun Lisa had learned to shoot with, the only one in fact that she'd ever fired. Staring at it in the box, she felt a hard knot of pain in her stomach.

She didn't want this. It went against everything she believed in. But she was also deeply frightened. Nagel's assurances were all well and good, but he hadn't lied to her. What he could do was limited, to say the least.

Slowly she lifted the gun out and looked at it. The weight of it was more than she remembered, but it seemed to be in good condition.

There were no bullets, of course. One of her father's most important rules had always been that guns were never kept loaded around the house.

She would have to buy bullets. There were plenty of stores around that sold them, but the idea of actually going into one made her hesitate.

She put the gun back in the box, relocked it carefully and returned the box to the closet. The key she kept with her.

Back downstairs, she went into the kitchen, poured the coffee down the sink and set about making a shopping list.

By noon, she'd done her errands. Her stomach rumbled but she ignored it. The last thing she wanted was food.

Just about then she remembered that she didn't have anything for Jimmy's dinner. In the grocery store, she picked up some chicken legs and a package of broccoli.

As she was leaving, she ran into Jane. "Still on the health food kick, I see," Lisa said. She even smiled, which considering how the day had been going so far, wasn't bad.

Jane laughed, but her eyes as they swept over her friend were serious. "Hey, I'll have you know that vanilla ice cream, hot dogs, potato chips and guacamole contain all the major food groups. Or at least the ones worth bothering with."

"You realize," Lisa teased, "that eating like that is a crime against nature. The only thing worse is getting away with it."

Jane shrugged. "What can I tell you, when they were handing out metabolisms, I was in the line for horses. So," she added, "how's it going?"

There'd never been much sense lying to Jane, she'd always seen through it. Besides, she already knew about Chas.

"Not so great," Lisa said. "Somebody's been watching my apartment in New York and I've been getting crank phone calls."

Jane's smile vanished. "What are you doing about it?" she demanded.

"I've talked to Sheriff Nagel. He's going to have the deputies check on the house. Beyond that, there's not much else he can do."

"I didn't ask about him," Jane said. "I said you. Have you talked to Mark?"

"Yes, as a matter of fact, I have."

"What does he say about it?"

Lisa frowned. Jane's instant assumption that Mark should be involved, that he could somehow help, was too close to the same instinct within herself. The one she was still fighting out of stubborn pride and an even more powerful fear of being hurt again.

Neither of which were helped by the memory of exactly what Mark had wanted her to do.

"He suggested I stay at his place," she admitted reluctantly. Quickly she added, "That was very generous but unnecessary."

Jane gave her a long level look that managed to suggest that she was not terribly bright. She pushed her groceries closer to the cash register and said, "Look, I'm not going to try to tell you what to do, but if that box in your pocketbook is what I think it is, you ought to reconsider. Sometimes it just doesn't pay to go it alone."

Lisa looked down quickly. Her purse was open. The box she'd bought at the gun store was plainly visible. She blanched and tugged the zipper closed.

"It's nothing."

Jane handed the clerk a twenty, pocketed her change, and slung the bag of groceries onto her hip. In a perfectly level voice, she said, "Honey, you were always the furthest thing from a fool, but there's times you've been just a little naive. If this is what you think it is—if Chas is involved—you *can't* go it alone."

"The sheriff..."

"Will do what he can under the law. He'll try, he really will. But Mark...Mark will do what he has to."

"So will I," Lisa said. Her voice was low but strong.

Jane looked at her sympathetically. "You've been hurt. It happens to the best of us. The hardest thing in the world is to admit that you need help, especially when you think asking for it might get you hurt even more."

"It isn't that—" Lisa began only to stop. It *was* that, exactly.

Chas had been a charming, seductive man who had whirled her away into a dream of romance only to drop her into ice-cold reality. But compared to Mark, he seemed like a careless boy.

The man who had climbed out of a dismal childhood, fought his way to stardom and made his life on his own terms was vastly more formidable. The harm Chas had done to her emotions was nothing at all compared to what she sensed Mark could inflict.

Was it any wonder that her instincts told her to steer clear of him?

"I'll be fine," she insisted even as she wished desperately that she could believe it.

Jane waited while Lisa paid for her purchases and then walked with her to her car. She waited until Lisa had gotten in, then said, "I'm sorry if I came down so hard, but I really am worried about you. If you don't want to take Mark's offer, you know you can come and stay with me."

"I know," Lisa said softly.

"I mean it. I've got plenty of room and we could have a good time. Remember the sleep-overs we used to have?"

"You mean the no-sleep-overs? How could I forget?"

"Okay, so we were young and giddy. But isn't there a part of you that still wants to stay up all night, try every shade of nail polish there is, and gorge on popcorn?"

"Sure there is. I'd even bring the butter. But I think it ought to wait."

"You're really determined to handle this by yourself?" Jane asked softly.

"I'm determined to protect Jimmy. That's what counts."

Jane stepped back from the car. She balanced the groceries on her hip and pushed aside the hair that had blown into her eyes. The weather had cleared but a stiff breeze was blowing off the lake to the north.

"Just so long as you promise you'll admit it if you get in over your head and you won't wait to do something about it."

"Promise," Lisa said. Moments later she pulled away from the curb. In the rearview mirror, she could see Jane staring after her, a look of deep concern etched on her friend's face.

What she didn't see was the nondescript, black four-door sedan that followed several car lengths behind her.

Chapter 12

Somewhat to her surprise, Lisa did manage to get some work done. The program she was working on might not be the most exciting in the world, but it did provide at least a brief break from the worries that seemed to be closing in around her.

It wasn't until a few minutes before she was due to pick up Jimmy that she switched off the computer, carried her coffee cup downstairs, and headed back outside to the car.

That was when she saw it. The black sedan was parked directly across from the house. There were two men in it. They were both dressed in business suits.

Except for a difference in their ages—one looked to be in his forties, the other was closer to thirty—they appeared cut from the same mold. Well-groomed, essentially faceless men of the kind who used to turn up on the old G-man shows, flashing badges and fighting for justice.

Only this time she was willing to bet that they were on the other side. Or maybe no side at all. Maybe they were among the breed that counted professionalism above all else, no sides, no causes, no ethics, never any notion of right or wrong. Just business.

That, more than anything that had gone before, terrified her.

She thought of the gun. It was still in the locked box in the bedroom closet. The bullets were hidden behind the toilet tank in her bathroom. She could go inside and get both. She could . . .

This was crazy. What was she thinking of? They were just two men sitting in a car. Even if they were watching her, she had to be slipping into the deep end to even consider such an action.

All right, no gun. She could go over to the car and confront them, demand to know what they were doing there.

And then what? They'd have some explanation, she was sure of that. Waiting for someone, looking for something, visitors to town, sightseeing, getting a little fresh air, anything. They would be cool, slightly puzzled by her curiosity, or perhaps not. Perhaps they wouldn't even bother to lie.

She could call Nagel. That, at least, made sense.

They were looking straight at her. Neither had moved, they weren't trying to conceal themselves in any way. They just sat there and stared at her.

She turned and went back into the house. There was a small amount of pride in the fact that she didn't run. She even shut the door quietly behind her.

Then she grabbed the phone, punched in the sheriff's number, and waited.

The call seemed to take forever to go through. She waited, heart rushing, through one ring...two rings.

"Sheriff's office."

"I need to speak to him...please, right away. It's Lisa Morley."

Silence for a moment before the young but reassuring voice said, "Hold on a minute, miss."

Silence again, dragging out, ten heartbeats, fifteen, seconds passing. Her mouth was dry. She swallowed with difficulty.

"Miss Morley? Nagel here. What's the problem?"

"There are two men in a black sedan parked across the street from my house."

"Ever seen them before?"

"No, I haven't."

"Are they doing anything besides just sitting there?"

"Anything else...?"

"Do you see a camera?"

"No, they're just watching."

"Okay," Nagel said crisply. "I'm putting a deputy on the line. You stay right where you are. A car's on the way."

She took a deep breath, fighting the fear. It was going to be all right. Maybe the men in the car were pros, but so was Nagel. He knew what to do. Someone would be there soon.

In fact, the patrol car pulled up beside the black sedan in less than three minutes. The cord on the kitchen phone was just long enough for her to carry it over to the side window and peer out. Two young officers emerged. They walked over to the black sedan, one on each side, and bent down slightly to talk to the men inside.

The conversation lasted several minutes. Both men in the sedan reached into their pockets and produced identification. The officers studied them. They asked a few more questions before returning the IDs. One walked back to the patrol car.

Minutes later, Nagel took the deputy's place on the phone.

"Their names are Sorenson and Deavers. Their licenses say they're both from New Jersey. The car's a rental. According to them, they're tourists, just passing through. They say they stopped where they are to look at a map."

"Do you believe that?" Lisa asked.

"Not necessarily. Unfortunately I can't prove they're lying. There's nothing illegal about stopping to look at a map."

"You know there has to be more to it than that. It's too much of a coincidence after what happened in New York." She spoke quickly, desperately worried that Nagel was going to dismiss her concern after all.

But instead he said, "I'm inclined to agree with you. The deputies are telling Mr. Sorenson and Mr. Deavers that this a real peaceful town where people look out for each other. We're letting them know that strangers stick out like a sore thumb. If they've got any brains at all, they'll get the message."

"Which is?"

"That anything they may have planned is going to boomerang right back on them."

Lisa bit her lower lip hard. She understood what he was saying. He wanted to reassure her without being misleading. She just wished the message wasn't so clear.

"Boomerang *after* it's happened, isn't that what you mean?"

Nagel sighed. He sounded like a man who wasn't too happy with himself just then. "What can I say? We used to have an anti-loitering law in this town, but it was struck down years ago. That means my hands are tied, at least to a certain extent. I can tell them they're being watched, that if they try anything, they'll be caught. But I can't go much further than that."

"So they've got a right to sit out there, watching me?" Lisa demanded. She was getting angry now.

"I'm afraid that's correct."

"What about my rights? Living without fear, keeping Jimmy safe? What about all that?"

"I'm sorry," Nagel replied. "Several states have instituted anti-stalking laws recently, but we don't happen to be one of them. The legislation is still pending."

"Pending?" Lisa repeated disbelievingly. "You're saying that these men can follow me around all they want to and because the law to stop them is *pending* you can't do anything about it?"

"I can if they directly threaten you in any way."

"They're threatening me by sitting outside my house watching me! Am I the only one who's getting that?"

"No," Nagel said quietly. His tone was genuinely regretful. "I've already ordered increased patrols around your house. We're on a limited budget, of course, but we'll do everything we possibly can."

"What if it isn't enough? What then?"

"We do our best, that's all I can tell you."

Angrily, Lisa said, "You mean you pick up the pieces. That's it, isn't it?"

Nagel sighed deeply. "There are times I don't like this job very much. This is one of them. Look, I'm giving it to you straight. We'll do everything we can, but it may not be enough. You want more than that, you know what you have to do."

"I know... ?"

"Go to Fletcher. I'm saying this off the record, Miss Morley, but I'm saying it loud and clear all the same. If you really think that your safety is on the line—or your boy's—then you go to Mark Fletcher. He can protect you a whole lot better than I can."

Lisa bit her lip again. It hurt but she didn't notice. "That's not the way things are supposed to be, Sheriff. We're supposed to have institutions to protect us, not have to rely on individuals."

"That's a nice ideal, but the reality doesn't always work the way we'd like. Mark Fletcher is the toughest man I happen to know. He's also the most decent. And he wants to help. You remember that."

She wouldn't soon forget it, Lisa thought as she hung up the phone. As if Mark hadn't been in her mind enough, Nagel had put him there front and center.

The toughest man. The most decent. Wants to help. The words echoed deep inside her even as she forced herself to go back outside. The black sedan was still there, but this time the two men were staring straight ahead. Defiantly, she got into her car. As she passed the sedan, she heard the engine start up.

They stayed a discreet distance behind, but there was no mistaking their intent. By the time she reached Nancy's house, her hands were shaking from a combination of fear and anger. Twice, a patrol car passed her, the officer slowing down, making sure the men in the sedan saw him, too. It made no difference. They parked half a block away as she got out and walked quickly up the path to the house.

Nancy frowned when she saw her. "Honey, you're not looking so good."

"I'm all right," Lisa said tautly. "Where's Jimmy?" She knew she was being rude and she hated it, but courtesy was being burned away along with almost everything else. All that mattered now was safety.

"He's in the playroom," Nancy replied at once. "You come on over here. You can see him right through the door. Sit down. I'm going to fix you a cup of tea."

"No. Please . . . I'm sorry, but I don't have time."

"All right," Nancy said slowly. "If you're in a rush, I understand."

A rush, Lisa thought. She squeezed her eyes shut for a moment, opened them to find Nancy watching her. A rush to where? Going back to the house would accomplish nothing. Neither would leaving Langston.

She had to make a stand. But to do it alone, with only the minimal help the police could give . . . She thought of the gun again and shivered.

Nancy's hand was warm and firm on her arm. "Honey, you really ought to sit down."

"No," Lisa said. Her voice was faint. The happy shouts of children filtered in from the playroom. Time

seemed to slow down. She was vividly aware of the
rays of sunshine coming through the windows, the familiar smell of cookies and furniture polish, the
strength of Nancy so close to her.

A woman's strength. Great enough to defy the
world, but also wise enough to know when the battle
can't be won alone.

Quietly, hearing her voice as though from a great
distance, she said, "I need to make a call."

Chapter 13

It took Mark less than ten minutes to reach Nancy MacEnroe's house. Considering that his spread was a good fifteen miles outside of town and he'd been in his office working when the call came, that suggested he hadn't wasted any time.

Nor did he come alone. The back of the pickup truck held no fewer than six very large, very determined-looking men.

Lisa was standing out in front of Nancy's house when he arrived. Their conversation on the phone had been brief. She'd wanted to explain more, but Mark seemed to feel that he didn't need to know anything beyond the fact that there were two men in a black sedan following her and that Sheriff Nagel couldn't do much about it.

She was waiting impatiently, hoping to have a word with him in private. But when he got out of the pickup, he barely glanced in her direction before starting off down the street toward the sedan.

His men followed. So did Lisa.

Mark walked up to the sedan, stopped and looked at it. He was wearing the usual plaid work shirt and jeans. His thick hair was ruffled by the breeze and he looked as though he'd been working outside most of the day. He seemed perfectly relaxed, even friendly. A slight smile played around his mouth as he studied the car.

His men joined him. The pair in the sedan glanced from side to side. The one behind the wheel said something. Unlike Mark, he didn't look pleased by the situation.

Mark's smile deepened. He didn't say a word, merely bent down and closed his large hands around the front fender of the car. His men fanned out in a circle.

"On three," Mark said casually.

"Three."

He lifted. So did the others. The sedan came up off the ground and hung several inches in the air. Maintaining his hold, Mark started walking to his left.

Smoothly, without so much as a ripple, the other men did the same. The pair behind the wheel were twisting back and forth, shouting, but Lisa was hardly aware of them. She simply watched, fascinated, as the sedan was turned completely around and set back down pointed in the opposite direction.

Mark dusted his hands off. He looked down at the two men in the car. "You boys got things a little mixed up. *That's* the way out of town."

The man behind the wheel—Sorenson or Deavers, it didn't matter which—gaped. His eyes were wide open, almost bulging. His face was red and his mouth twisted in a snarl.

"Who the hell do you think you are?" he demanded.

Mark gave a little shake of his head, as though realizing that he'd been remiss. "Guess I should have introduced myself. I'm a friend of Lisa Morley's."

He gestured to the big, grinning men around him. So far as they were concerned, this was fun. "As a matter of fact, we all are. You could say this is a real friendly town, at least for the right people."

The driver still looked badly shaken but he was also fighting it. Sneering, he said, "Tough guy. How do you suppose you'd do alone, buddy? Just you and me, one on one."

Mark bared his teeth. "Get out of the car and we'll find out." He took hold of the door handle.

Lisa held her breath. The man was clearly tempted. He'd been humiliated and he wanted something of his own back for it. But he also had enough sense to realize that he'd be in for the fight of his life.

All the men around the car were very large, heavily muscled, with the broad-shouldered, lean-hipped look of men who took hard work as a normal part of life. But none of them radiated the sense of danger that Mark did.

He stood with his feet planted slightly apart, hands hanging loosely at his sides, seemingly at ease yet clearly ready for anything. Perhaps even hoping for it.

"Come on," he said softly. "Just you and me. Leave the woman and the kid out of it. What do you say?"

"I say you're crazy," the other man interrupted suddenly. He was the older of the two and, for the moment at least, apparently the wiser. "Come on, let's get out of here."

The driver shot Mark a final glare and turned on the car, stomping on the gas pedal. The sedan shot off down the street, tires squealing. Behind it, the six men broke into gales of laughter. Mark merely smiled.

He strolled over to Lisa and said, "Haven't done that since high school."

She stared at him in disbelief. "This wasn't the first time?"

"Heck, no. Car turning's a fine old sport. It's a variation on car moving. We used to do that, too."

"Why?" Lisa asked.

He shrugged and managed to look just a little abashed. "It's a guy thing. Where are your car keys?"

"Right here," she said.

He took them from her and before she could stop him, tossed the keys to one of his men. "Bring the car, Sam."

"Wait a minute," Lisa said. "I didn't mean for you to—"

"You can ride in the truck," Mark said, going right over her protest as though it didn't exist. "Jimmy'll like that."

It was true, he would. But that wasn't exactly the point. "Look, I really appreciate your coming and the way you handled this but—"

"I didn't handle anything," Mark interrupted quietly. He stopped walking and stood there looking at her through ice-blue eyes. "All I did was give those two goons something to think about. That doesn't mean they won't be back. In fact, they'll probably bring reinforcements."

"Maybe not. Maybe they'll—"

His hands closed on her shoulders gently but with the unmistakable message that enough was enough. "Honey, you're a brave woman and I respect that. But you've got to face facts. You against them just isn't fair. All I'm asking is that you let me tip the odds in your favor. Now that's not a whole lot, is it?"

Not the way he put it, especially not when that deep, rough-velvet voice wrapped itself around her and made all the rest of the world seem to fade away down a long tunnel going nowhere. Not a whole lot at all.

No doubt about it, she was going down for the third time, but she wasn't doing it without a struggle.

"Just how," she asked on a thread of sound, "do you mean to do that?"

"The same way I said before. You and Jimmy move into my place. I've got thirty men working full time and they all know how to keep their eyes open. You'll be safe there, I promise."

Behind her, she heard Sam start up her car. Events were rushing beyond her control. Chas, the men, Mark, it was all piling on top of her faster than she could handle.

Only one thing stood out sharply and clearly—she had to protect Jimmy. Her own feelings—and fears—didn't count for anything next to that.

Softly she said, "It seems as though I don't have a choice."

Mark's hands tightened for an instant before he caught himself. He let her go but he stayed close. His expression was hard, unreadable.

"No," he said, "you don't."

Chapter 14

Jimmy was asleep. He'd fought to stay awake, but finally his hazel eyes had drifted shut, the long lashes fanning out over his cheeks, and his breathing becoming slow and regular.

Lisa tucked the covers more snugly around him. He nestled against her, clutching his bear, without a care in the world. But then why would he be otherwise?

They'd had hamburgers, potato chips and ice cream for dinner. Worse yet, she couldn't swear Mark had done it on purpose. A glance in the refrigerator had convinced her that he was definitely a meat and potatoes man. If she really was going to stay there, a quick trip to the vegetable store was a top priority.

Naturally, Jimmy had been delighted. In Mark's company, he seemed suddenly older, less the little boy and more some other unknown creature in the process of being formed.

They'd talked about hockey. To the best of her knowledge, Jimmy had never seen a hockey game in his life. Yet after a two-minute explanation of the rules that went completely over her head but apparently made perfect sense to her son, he proceeded to bombard Mark with a steady stream of questions, all of them patiently answered. It had been topped off finally by a trip into Mark's office so Jimmy could actually hold in his own two hands the hockey stick taken down from the wall for just that purpose.

Little boy heaven.

Now he was blissfully asleep in a bed he'd never slept in before, in a room he hadn't ever seen until that afternoon, under the roof of a man he barely knew and yet who was indisputably filling a gaping hole in his life.

Slowly, Lisa stood up. She smoothed Jimmy's hair, dropped a light kiss on his forehead, and tiptoed out of the room.

It wasn't quite nine o'clock. After leaving Nancy's, they'd stopped at Lisa's house long enough for her to pack her belongings. Her computer was already set up in a spare bedroom. Her suitcase was in another, right next to Jimmy's room.

If she wanted to, she could go to bed. Or she could try to work. Neither option had much appeal.

She was far too tense to sleep. By the same token, she shuddered to think what any computer code she might try to write would look like.

She could go for a walk, except she didn't know her way around the farm very well. Beyond the circle of light that surrounded the house and closest outbuildings, the darkness was complete.

She could try to find something to read. Besides the hockey stick, there was an entire wall of books in Mark's office. Surely they didn't all deal with sports or farming.

Or she could do what she knew she ought to, which was to remember that she was a guest in this house and that any attempt to avoid her host would be at the very least rude, not to mention undoubtedly futile.

Mark wasn't exactly the sort of man she could overlook. Even now, standing in the hallway outside Jimmy's room, she was vividly aware of him nearby. The soft crackle and pop of the logs in the great room's fireplace grew louder as she hesitantly approached.

He was there, sitting on the oversized leather sofa just as he'd been when she excused herself to put Jimmy to bed. He faced the fire, one long leg resting on the other, apparently immersed in the book he was reading.

Lisa stopped just within the entrance to the room and studied him. The rough-hewn, straight-shooting, take-no-prisoners man from the afternoon was gone. In his place was a relaxed, somewhat pensive, gentlemanly looking fellow engrossed in his reading before the crackling fire.

The clothes were the same—jeans and work shirt—and the features revealed by the play of light and shadow hadn't changed. He was the same man who had confronted Sorenson and Deavers with a flat-out threat wrapped in cutting mockery. The man who had told her in no uncertain terms that she was going to accept his protection whether she wanted to or not. The man who had showed Jimmy how to flip hamburgers and had let him spoon out the ice cream. Who sent shivers down her spine and made her knees feel weak.

A soft breath of sound escaped her. He looked up, straight into her eyes.

"Everything all right?"

"Fine," she murmured. Taking a firm grip on herself, she came the rest of the way into the room and sat down on the couch opposite him. "Jimmy's asleep."

Mark smiled. The lines deepened around his eyes. "He looked done in."

"Big day. Actually, a whole bunch of them. He's been through a lot."

"But he seems to be doing fine." Mark put the book aside. He got up and poked at the fire. Sparks flew up the chimney as the scent of birch filled the room.

"You ought to be proud of that," he said as he sat down again. He was leaning forward, his arms resting on his knees. It was very quiet in the room.

"I haven't thought much about it," Lisa admitted. She spoke automatically, hardly aware of what she was saying.

When had she last been with a man in such a tranquil and undemanding setting? After Chas, she'd had no inclination to date anyone. Even with him, there had been so few such evenings that she could probably count them on one hand, if she could remember them at all. He simply hadn't been the domestic sort.

She wouldn't have thought Mark was either. Certainly his earlier years had done nothing to suggest he'd be other than a heartbreaker. Yet here he was, seeming content with hearth and home. It was a transformation she could still hardly believe.

"We need to talk," she said quietly.

Mark sighed. He looked resigned, as though he'd been expecting this. "How about in the morning after you've had some sleep?"

After a night under his roof, protected by him, in a bed just down the hall from his own? No, she didn't think so.

"I'd rather do it now." For courtesy's sake, she added, "If you wouldn't mind?"

She girded herself, thinking he'd argue, or maybe just try to bulldoze her as he'd done earlier. But instead he surprised her.

"All right," he said. "What do you want to talk about?"

"This." She moved her hand in a gesture that encompassed her surroundings. "The situation."

"Oh," Mark said as he leaned back more comfortably. A hint of amusement danced in his eyes. "That."

"I'd just like to clarify a few things," Lisa insisted. He might find it amusing, but she didn't. The sooner they got some ground rules down, the better.

"I can see why you're good with computers. You like to dot the *t's* and cross the *i's*, don't you?"

Despite herself, Lisa smiled. "That's dot the *i's* and cross the *t's.*"

"See now, that's why I'll never get much further with computers than asking them how much money I made this month."

"As long as you like the answers you get, that should be enough. And speaking of money, while Jimmy and I are here I really think I should pay our expenses."

"No. Now what's the next thing you want to clarify?"

Lisa's cheeks warmed. He spoke with perfect amiability, but there was no mistaking the undercurrent of steel. Her resolve strengthened.

"Wait a minute, you're not going to brush me off just like that. I'm serious."

"So am I, and I'm not trying to brush you off. There's just no way I'm going to waste my time figuring out how many pancakes Jimmy ate or how many showers you took. It's not worth it."

"I can't just take advantage of your hospitality. It isn't right."

Mark sighed. He thought for a moment. "I'll tell you what, if it means that much to you, you can work out the bugs in a program that's supposed to help me manage feed portions but seems to think I'm trying to grow chickens, not cows. Okay?"

"I should be able to do that," Lisa agreed. She was relieved that there was something she could do to repay at least a small portion of what he'd done for her. But she didn't fool herself, debugging a program by no means balanced the scales.

"Please don't think I'm ungrateful," she said softly, "just because I want to do something in return. There's really no way I can adequately thank you for the help you've given Jimmy and me."

His mouth hardened. Flatly he said, "I don't need any thanks. You've got a problem, I can provide a solution. That's all there is to it."

"There are people who wouldn't see it that way."

He stood up again, unfolding his long, powerful body from the couch. She watched as he walked over to the wet bar, opened it and took out a bottle of club soda.

"Would you like a drink?" he asked.

She stood up, too, suddenly aware of the quiet all around them and the way time was slipping past. "No, thank you. I'm pretty tired, actually. I thought I'd turn in."

He nodded and splashed soda into a glass. "You have everything you need?"

"Yes, thank you." She hesitated. Half the width of the room was between them and yet she felt caught within the circle of his strength and confidence, the sheer male power of him unlike anything she had ever really known. She swayed slightly and had to catch hold of herself.

"Go to bed," Mark said, almost harshly. Catching himself, he added, "It's been a long day."

She nodded. Her lips were dry. "Yes, it has been." One step toward the hall, another. She could do this, she could walk away. It just wasn't very easy. "Good night."

From the shadows, softly caressing, his voice touched her. "Good night, Lisa. Sleep well."

Chapter 15

To her surprise, Lisa did. She slept clear through to morning, waking to cloudless skies and birds singing outside her windows. For several minutes she lay on her back staring up at the ceiling, trying to order her thoughts.

Only gradually did she become aware that the light was brighter than she was accustomed to seeing when she woke. This wasn't the soft, slanting sun of dawn. This was the strong sun of morning well on its way.

Quickly she sat up and looked at the clock on the table beside the bed. A soft gasp escaped her. It was almost ten a.m. She couldn't remember the last time she had slept so late. Certainly not since before having Jimmy.

Jimmy. Where was he? What was he doing?

Jumping from the bed, she grabbed her robe and pulled it on as she hurried to the door. The hallway beyond was empty. So was Jimmy's room.

Her heart speeded up. She reached the great room and stood there, looking all around, uncertain what direction to go in.

From outside, laughter reached her. Sweet, pleasant, familiar laughter. Through the window she saw Jimmy playing with a dog that was almost as big as he was. They were rolling around on the lawn, a bundle of wagging tail, lolling tongue and little-boy shrieks of pleasure.

Her shoulders slumped in relief. She went back to her room and dressed quickly in slacks and a loose cotton sweater. A few quick swipes with a hairbrush, a splash of cold water to her face, and she was ready.

Back outside, Jimmy was throwing a stick for the dog to fetch. The rough-haired animal—a cross between a German shepherd and a collie—caught it in midair and trotted back, tail high, to drop the stick at Jimmy's feet. The boy threw his arms around the dog's neck just as Lisa stepped out onto the porch.

"Wow, did you see that, Mommy? Isn't he great?"

"The greatest," Lisa said softly. It occurred to her that she couldn't remember ever seeing Jimmy play with a dog. They hadn't been allowed to have pets in the building where they'd lived and the few dogs who were brought to the nearby park were kept firmly leashed.

She went down the steps and walked over to where he was standing. Kneeling beside him, she asked, "Have you been up long?"

Jimmy nodded proudly. "Hours and hours. I got dressed myself and then I helped Mark make breakfast. We had waffles."

"Sounds delicious."

"I was going to wake you up so you could have some, but Mark said you probably needed to sleep. He said we could have them for dinner if you want. Can we?"

"We'll see. Is Mark around?"

"He had to go into town. He said I should stay here 'cause you'd wake up pretty soon."

A figure emerged from the barn that was catercorner to the house, separated by the lawn and a line of trees. Lisa straightened. She recognized one of the men from the previous afternoon.

He came over, wiping his forehead with a handkerchief, and nodded pleasantly. "Morning, ma'am. Mr. Fletcher had to go into town." He grinned at Jimmy and cocked his head toward the barn. "Me and Hank been keeping an eye on your boy."

To Jimmy, he said, "Nice job you did on the milking, sport. You can help again tomorrow if the boss says it's okay." As an afterthought, he added, "And your mom, too."

"Can I, Mom?"

Milking? "We'll see." She was overusing that all-purpose answer, but at the moment it was the only one she could come up with. "Thank you for your help... It's Sam, isn't it?"

He nodded, pleased that she'd remembered. "That's right, ma'am. No trouble at all. He's a good kid."

Sam went on back to the barn and Jimmy returned to playing with the dog. "Am I going to Mrs. Mac-Enroe's today?" he asked, his voice half muffled in fur.

Lisa hesitated. She didn't want to make him feel like a prisoner, but neither did she feel safe taking him back into town until she knew for sure that the men were gone. "Do you want to?" she asked.

"It's nice there, but I really like it here, too. Sam said later on if Mark says it's okay, maybe I could try out a pony they've got." He was silent for a moment, mulling things over, before he asked, "Is Mark the boss?"

"I guess so," Lisa murmured. There seemed little point in trying to deny it. "I'm going to get a cup of coffee. Will you be all right out here?"

He shot her a look that was at once disbelieving and tolerant. "Sure. Bandit and me are going to play some more."

The dog grinned, tail beating furious time. The name suited him. He had stolen Jimmy's heart. Lisa couldn't blame him for it.

Jimmy looked happier than she'd seen him in a long time. She watched as he raced across the lawn, sturdy legs flashing in the sun and the big dog chasing after him, both looking as though they were having the time of their lives.

With a sigh, she went back into the house. The kitchen was in the back. It was a big, spacious room with yellow walls, long oak counters and the latest appliances.

There was a note on the refrigerator door. "Gone into town. Back about 5:00 p.m. Anything you need, ask Sam." It was followed by the dark slash of Mark's signature.

There was also a thermos of fresh coffee on the counter. Lisa poured a cup and drank part of it as she stared absently out the window.

Only gradually did she become aware that something was missing. The house was quiet. Far in the distance, she could hear the muted sounds of farm equipment working. Closer by, faint laughter and the sound of Bandit barking reached her.

Sunlight filtered through the high windows. It was a beautiful, peaceful day. A day without any immediate worry or crisis to drain her. No phone calls, no watching men, no fear for Jimmy or herself.

Until then, she hadn't admitted how much such fear had weighed her down. It had seeped into her very soul, draining her of energy and her usual optimistic view of life.

But not now. Suddenly she was almost giddily free. So of course what was she going to do? Work, what else?

A definite feeling of pleasure went through her as she settled in front of the computer. The fact was she liked what she did for a living. Normally she found it challenging and rewarding. It was only recently that everything had taken on a dark and difficult cast. With that gone, she was able to get a great deal done in just a few hours.

She took a break for lunch with Jimmy, listening gladly to all his exploits of the morning, and then went back to work. From the window of the room she was using, she could see him playing with Bandit. He came in once to ask if it was okay to go for a tractor ride with Sam. When she said it was, he raced off.

By midafternoon, she was well caught up and ready to call it a day. After being assured by Sam and several other of the men that Jimmy was absolutely not in the way and that they were all having a great time together, she decided on a belated shower.

An hour later, considerably refreshed but feeling a little at loose ends, she surveyed the few clothes she had with her. Doing the laundry was definitely going to be a priority. In the meantime, she pulled out a dress she hadn't worn in a while and dropped it over her head.

The dress was a soft calico print in mauve and lavender with a scoop neck, long sleeves, and a skirt that reached almost to her ankles. She'd bought it in an uncharacteristically whimsical moment and had brought it along because it was easy to take care of. Besides, she was tired of pants.

That done, she went back outside to reclaim her happy but very dirty son. He came reluctantly, still brimming over with excitement. Bandit came, too, flopping down in front of the fireplace in a way that made it clear he felt perfectly at home.

While Jimmy splashed in the bathtub, Lisa surveyed the kitchen. Mark had said he would be back by five and it was getting on for that. She found a container of stew in the freezer and set it in the microwave to thaw as she began setting the table.

Mark came in just as she was finishing. He looked tired, dusty, and almost indescribably attractive.

Lisa set the last plate in place, straightened a napkin a fraction of an inch, and mustered a smile. She felt ridiculously self-conscious.

"How was your day?" she asked.

Absently he said, "Fine. Everything all right here?"

"Sure, it's been great. By the way, thank you for letting Jimmy spend time with Sam and the others. He's really enjoyed it."

"I told them to keep an eye on him. You needed to get some work done, right?"

She nodded, realized she was staring at him and forced herself to look away. Big, gorgeous, sexy, tender, considerate, protective *and* he respected the fact that she worked. Heaven help her.

"Dinner's almost ready," she murmured.

He looked surprised. "You didn't have to do that."

"I don't mind."

He hesitated, standing in the door of the kitchen, his shoulders almost filling it. Although the day was mild, his blue cotton work shirt clung to him. Dirt streaked his forehead.

"Do I have time to get cleaned up?"

She nodded again, suddenly not trusting herself to speak and feeling all the more ridiculous for that. It was all so sweetly normal. She would have been perfectly at home in a frilly apron.

He went, after another long look at her, and she inhaled deeply, hoping to steady her nerves. It didn't work. Out in the hall beyond the kitchen, she heard Jimmy.

"Mark's back!"

"I know, honey..." She turned, intending to tell him dinner would be ready soon, only to be confronted by the dripping, mostly naked Peter Pan-like figure of her son clad in underpants, socks and a few stray bubbles.

"Go finish getting dressed," she admonished him as she grabbed a towel and bent to wipe up the water.

"I gotta talk to Mark. I have to ask him about the pony." His voice trailed off down the hall as he charged, full tilt, toward Mark's room.

"He's busy," Lisa yelled. "Wait until din—"

Too late. A door slammed and then another. Voices mingled, her son's high eagerness and the deeper, calmer resonance in response.

She would go and apologize for Jimmy's bad manners. She would explain that he had to respect Mark's privacy. She'd bring him back—by the scruff of his neck if she had to—get him dressed and set him to some task.

Laughter rose, a boy's and a man's. It sounded...what, exactly? Friendly but more. Faintly conspiratorial. As though they were, the two of them, bound in ways she couldn't understand.

Let it go, her mind said. Save the apologies and the admonitions for later.

Good advice, she knew, yet it took all her willpower to walk back into the kitchen, leaving her son in that male world he had so clearly yearned for and which she could never enter.

They joined her in the kitchen half an hour later, both freshly scrubbed and fully dressed. Jimmy had on his khaki pants, the same as Mark's. He'd even found his denim shirt, again the same, *and* had buttoned it correctly.

"Mommy doesn't know how to shave," he was saying as they entered. "Mark showed me," he informed her. "You have to use soap."

"Useful to know," Lisa murmured under her breath. Her chest was tight. He looked so completely happy.

"Here," Mark said softly as he came to stand beside her. He took the oven mitts from her hands and reached for the stew pot. "I'll take care of that."

He set the pot on the table. Lisa followed with the bread and salad. Out of the corner of her eye, she saw Mark shoot Jimmy a look. Her son leaped forward and pulled out her chair.

Chapter 16

A clown on stilts walked past, painted grin beaming and a gaggle of children in his wake. Jugglers, gymnasts, magicians and spangled ladies abounded and everywhere the barkers filled the night air with their prattle.

"Three rings for a quarter. Try your luck! Right here, three for a quarter! Step right up, sir. Win a prize."

"One dollar—one dollar only!—gets you ten turns at the ball. Try your luck, show off your skill. That's it, ma'am, put it right through that hoop and pick your prize!"

"Who's the strongest he-man in Langston? You show us! Right here, right now. No tricks, just raw power! You got it, let's see it!"

"Panda bears, Kewpie dolls, toys for the kids, hit the bull's-eye, win 'em all! One dollar, one dollar only!"

"Get your cotton can-dy!"

"Bal-loons, right here!"

"Hot dogs, foot-long hot dogs! Get 'em while they last!"

The smells of sizzling food, spun sugar, soda syrup, mustard and all the rest mingled with the heady aromas of straw, exhaust, animals and the ineffable something that was pure excitement. Colors spun before the eye in a swirling patchwork of satin and khaki, glitter and plaid carousing under the velvet sky. Through it all, the calliope music soared, drawing the crowd inward down the ranks of booths and tents to the magic circle where festooned horses galloped.

Jimmy made a beeline for the carousel. Mark and Lisa followed a bit more sedately. They had decided after dinner to visit the carnival again now that it was officially open.

Most of Langston seemed to be doing the same. People surged around them as they found a place next to the railing around the carousel.

Lisa was pressed close against Mark. Through the thin cotton dress she wore, she was vividly aware of his size and strength. The night was cool, but the warmth of his body reached out to envelop her. She stood, staring straight ahead at her son, smiling automatically even as her senses tumbled over each other.

She was glad to be out of the house. The intimacy over dinner, subtle as it had been, had left her disoriented. She felt as though she had suddenly stepped out of her life—the one she knew and admittedly had helped to make—and into something altogether different.

Being at the carnival gave her some time out to try to pull herself together. Or so she had thought. In reality, she could think of little except the whirling lights and music, and beyond them all, of the man whose nearness overwhelmed all else.

The crowd grew even denser. Lisa was pushed against Mark. He put an arm around her protectively and turned just enough, drawing her into the shelter of his body.

"Better?" he asked. His voice sounded deep and slightly husky.

She nodded although that was a lie. Better was hardly what she was feeling.

The crowd eased just a little. She breathed a sigh of relief but didn't try to move beyond the circle of his arm. Instead she moved her head, tilting slightly, enough to find him gazing down at her with a look in his eyes she couldn't read.

"Lisa . . ."

She watched, fascinated, as his mouth shaped her name. The music drifted through her and away, growing fainter. The crowd became no more than a shadow surrounding them.

His head bent. She felt him hesitate a fraction of a second and in that tiny sliver of time raised herself so slightly, so very little but enough.

His lips were firm and warm. He didn't demand anything but touched gently, once, and then again, coaxing until with a soft moan she pressed closer and met his kiss with her own.

In the vast scheme of the world, it was of very small
import. Just a kiss, and not blatantly passionate at
that. But for her—and if she was any judge, for
Mark—it was far more.

Sunburst moments later as the calliope music began to slow, he raised his head and stared down at her.
His eyes were hooded, the lids slumberous. She swallowed hard and with difficulty tore her gaze away.

Her heart was beating very hard as Jimmy burst
through the gate, hurtling himself at them both.

"Can we go on the Ferris wheel now?" he asked.

Why not? Lisa thought. What better than to sit on
a giant wheel and be hurled between earth and stars?
It suited the situation perfectly.

Three rides later, Lisa's head was spinning almost as
much as the wheel itself. Mark cast her a quick glance
and quietly called a halt. Tellingly, Jimmy made no
attempt to change his mind.

"Looks like he's done in," Mark said. Gently he
lifted the boy. Jimmy's head dropped forward onto his
shoulder. He murmured drowsily.

When Lisa returned to the great room after putting
Jimmy to bed there was no sign of Mark. She didn't
know whether to be relieved or sorry. For a woman
who had been married and borne a child, the single
kiss they'd shared had had a startling impact on her.
She had only to let her thoughts drift to him—and they
did that of their own accord anyway—and she could
almost feel again the touch of his lips on hers. Her
breasts were unusually sensitive, the nipples pressing
against the lace of her bra and deep within she felt an
unaccustomed tightening.

A faint smile curved her lips. All things considered, it was probably just as well that Mark was making himself scarce. She would just tidy up a bit and then go to bed herself.

Compulsive neatness had never been her strong point but they had left so hurriedly for the carnival that the dinner dishes were still in the sink. Mark would probably be up first thing in the morning and she thought the least she could do was leave him a clean kitchen.

Besides, the simple ordinariness of the task helped settle her nerves, at least a little. It was hard to feel romantic while loading the dishwasher.

But not, as it turned out, impossible.

She was adding the soap when a sound behind her made her turn. Mark was standing at the back door. He looked surprised to see her.

"I thought you'd gone to bed," he said.

She shut the dishwasher door, locked it and flipped the on switch. "I thought you'd done the same."

The lines around his eyes deepened. "I guess we were both wrong."

She wiped her hands on a towel and hung it neatly on the rack beside the sink. "Well . . . it's late . . ."

He nodded but didn't move away from the door. His eyes ran over her, taking in the hair tousled by the night breeze, the cheeks slightly flushed, and the soft cotton shades of dream-laden clouds shaping to her slender figure.

Quietly he said, "Come outside for a moment. There's something you should see."

Don't think, her mind whispered, just act. She crossed the room, coming to him, and with her hand curled in his, stepped out into the night.

The sky was radiantly clear. A sickle moon hung over the fields, where new life stirred. But beyond it, drawing both eye and spirit, was the vast sea of stars.

Lisa gasped softly. She hadn't seen the stars so clearly since leaving Langston. Memory couldn't truly hold the image. She stood, head back, and drank it in, knowing that she was gazing into eternity.

"It's incredible," she murmured finally.

Mark nodded. "Nothing like the night sky for giving a person perspective. Look over there."

She followed the direction of his hand. There, high above the spreading oak trees, deep in the velvet darkness, diamonds spilled. Hundreds of them streaked past each other, more constantly appearing from an unseen source, raining down upon the silent earth.

"What . . . ?" Lisa murmured, awestruck.

"It's a meteor shower. They happen at this time of year."

"It's incredible. I've never seen anything like it."

"There *is* nothing like it," Mark said. "I saw the aurora borealis one time up in Canada. That was magnificent, but there's something about this . . ."

She nodded, not speaking now for the heavens had all her attention. For a time, they stood, close together, silent and watchful under the rain of stars. Until, so slowly, the warmth of their bodies grew against the coolness of the night and they were drawn closer still.

So close... eyes touching, the whisper of Mark's breath on her cheek, the brush of his hand on her skin, and the need growing, spreading through her, ever stronger until it became at last undeniable.

Her arms twined around his neck. She made a sound deep in her throat. The hard wall of his chest rubbed against her aching breasts. His hands moved down her back, stroking hungrily as his mouth claimed hers.

This time his kiss was hard and wild. Her lips parted beneath the searching pressure of his. She gasped softly as his tongue plunged, mating with hers. Deep tremors seized her. She clung more tightly to him as heat engulfed them both.

Sweet heaven but she wanted him. He made her feel more vividly alive than she could ever remember being. His strength engulfed her, at once demanding and protective. The roughness of his lean cheeks against her smooth skin, the iron hardness of his arms holding her, the unmistakable knowledge of his desire, all sent reason fleeing.

She moaned again as her head fell back, exposing the vulnerable line of her throat. His teeth raked the delicate skin lightly as his hands moved down her back to clasp her buttocks.

"Lisa," he murmured tautly, "I can't control this much longer. If you want me to stop, say so."

His bluntness pierced the dazzling veil of pleasure that enfolded her. The proof of his arousal pressed against her abdomen, urgent and demanding. Her breath faltered. One small word, that was all she had to say, and he would stop. Of that she had no doubt.

No matter how powerful the need she had unleashed, she trusted him completely.

One word, nothing more.

"Lisa..." he said again.

Her answer was to gather up all the fear and worry, the doubt and discouragement, all the years that had turned her from girl to woman and hurl them into the diamond sky.

"You talk too much," she said, and claimed his mouth with hers.

Chapter 17

He shouldn't do this.

The harsh truth of that lay like a stone-cold pain in Mark's gut even as all the rest of him threatened to explode with heat.

She was a woman on the run, fearful for her child's safety and possibly also her own. Few other circumstances could have made her more vulnerable. And that, most definitely, wasn't his style.

Vulnerable women had never appealed to him. He liked them tough, independent and feisty. Women who were out for a good time and didn't come with a whole lot of strings attached. Maybe it wasn't fair, but his favorite bedmates had always been women who tended to look on sex the same way a lot of men did—good exercise with an afterglow.

No matter how he tried, he couldn't see Lisa that way. Not even her sudden aggressiveness changed that.

There was a hint of desperation in the way she kissed him, in the silken press of her body against his, in the husky little sounds that came from her throat.

Not that all that wasn't incredibly sexy. It was. He was instantly, almost painfully aroused. The shock of it stunned him. He couldn't remember feeling like this since he was sixteen years old and he wasn't sure it had happened even then.

She had barely touched him, they were both fully dressed and he was—supposedly—smart enough to know better. But he was on fire for sweet Lisa Morley. There was just no getting around that.

Which didn't make it any righter.

Her lips brushed softly over his again, dancing lightly, almost tentatively. She hadn't even touched him with her tongue or done anything else that was all that erotic. Considering how he felt already, it was probably just as well. He doubted he could stand it.

His hands closed on her shoulders. He meant to pull away. That was his clear-cut intent, the choice he knew he had to make. He even took a deep breath, steadying himself as best he could to do it.

But the breath was flavored with her—honeysuckle soap and heaven-scent woman, new-mown grass and dappled starlight. He breathed again, raggedly, fighting for control.

He'd had women who were so skilled they could have turned pro. Hell, some of them probably had. Lisa, for all that she'd been married and had a child, was an innocent. Why was he so much more vulnerable to her merest touch?

Vulnerable. There it was again, only him this time, not just her. He'd been around the block a time or two himself and it hadn't always been fun. Much as he didn't like admitting it, the failure of his marriage had hit him hard, not because of any real feelings for his wife but because of what he'd wanted her to represent.

He'd been ready back then to take the plunge into marriage and family, respectability and responsibility. Ready? Hell, he'd been champing at the bit.

The day he came back to the overpriced house in the burbs crammed full of furniture he couldn't stand—and too often people he didn't even know—he'd been forced to reassess his plans. Not because there was any big crowd present, for once his wife hadn't been entertaining, but because she'd been playing to an audience of strictly one.

About the best that could be said was that the guy hadn't been a teammate. Mark had already been around long enough to know that even that kind of thing happened occasionally.

This time around it was—and he actually got some sick amusement from this—an accountant. While other women were going nuts for jocks, his little wifey had developed the hots for a bean counter.

Two months later the divorce papers were signed and a year later it was official. He found his solace in the slashing mayhem of the hockey rink, playing with more ruthless skill than ever before.

He got a reputation and he got the women, too. He used them just as they used him and he told himself he had no regrets. There was nothing more he wanted.

Until he climbed out of the truck on a rain-swept night and found a girl from his past looking straight at him.

Just a minute more and he'd call a halt. That wasn't so long, was it? In the overall scheme of things, it hardly counted at all. He hardly knew when his hand slipped up from her shoulder and around to the back of her head. He held her, his fingers thrusting into the feathery hair, as he struggled with all his considerable strength for the control that was fast fading.

Lisa drew back just a little. Her eyes met his. She looked dazed and about as surprised as he was.

"Mark...?"

He swallowed hard, still tasting her on his lips. Her cheeks were flushed and her mouth slightly swollen. He could feel the rapid rise and fall of her breasts against him. She shifted slightly and her flat stomach grazed his erection.

There were a lot of things he'd thought of saying, all amounting to how he really cared about her but he didn't think this was such a good idea...not right then...need more time...and so on.

He said none of it. Instead he looked into her green-gold eyes, the eyes that had seen him as a hurting boy and that gazed on him now as a man capable of stirring her to such dazzled passion, and said nothing at all.

Instead he acted. His head lowered, raven hair mingling with the velvet sky. His strength surrounded her, the rock hardness of his body drawing her implacably.

Her eyes fluttered shut, the lashes lying dark against petal-smooth skin. He bent, slipped an arm beneath her knees and walked determinedly back toward the house.

* * *

His room was at the far end of the first floor in a wing of its own that included a bath and a dressing area. Lisa had a quick, fleeting impression of stark white walls, paintings that were slashes of vivid color, dark, elegantly restrained furniture.

At the center of it all was a large platform bed covered in a vivid star-patterned quilt. Mark lowered her gently, sliding her down the length of his body. Without letting go of her, he yanked the covers back.

She hardly noticed. The sensations pouring through her blanked out almost everything else. Opposite the bed was a large, low dresser and above it a mirror in a simple silver frame. A woman stared out of it, flushed, full-mouthed and with slumberous eyes.

She shivered and tore her gaze away. It didn't matter who the stranger was, the person inside her she had never before recognized. Caution, fear, doubt, none of it counted. There was only this moment and the terrible, driving need that seemed to have swallowed her whole. If she didn't find relief from it soon . . .

"You ever notice," Mark said huskily, "how in the movies, they skip over this part?" He was hopping on one foot, yanking off a boot. The other followed quickly.

She laughed, suddenly happy in a way she didn't really understand but was smart enough not to question. Looking him straight in the eye, she said, "Somehow, I think we'll manage."

They did. The buttons of his shirt gave way to reveal the broad, solid expanse of his chest, sculpted with muscle. His skin was burnished and lightly dusted with dark whorls of hair that thickened as it ran in a straight line down over his stomach to disappear in the band of his jeans.

Lisa followed it tentatively with the tip of one finger, savoring the springy feel. His breathing grew harsh.

"Do you know what you're doing to me?" he asked.

"I'm not sure." Tremors ran through her. Her breasts felt heavier, the nipples full and aching. "But if it feels anything like I'm feeling, then . . ."

"Then we're a pretty good match," he murmured, and slid both his hands up over her hips and buttocks. The soft cotton dress buttoned down the front. His fingers moved with some difficulty. He cursed under his breath.

"Damn it, everything about you is so delicate."

Her head moved back with surprise. She never thought of herself that way. "Here," she said, covering his hands with her own, guiding him as one by one the buttons yielded.

"The way I feel," he said thickly as he looked at her, "I could have just ripped them off, but that's such a pretty dress and I've got the feeling you don't wear it too often."

The tip of her tongue moistened her lips. She was suddenly acutely self-conscious. With the front of her dress spread open, the thin lacy bra she wore hid little.

She glanced down, seeing herself for an instant as he did, all smooth glowing skin, her breasts full and the nipples swelling against scraps of lace. A shiver ran through her.

"Cold?" he asked.

She shook her head, not trusting herself to speak. He smiled thinly as though the effort was almost beyond him. "God, you're beautiful."

Slowly she slid her hands along his shoulders, slipping the shirt down his arms. He shrugged it off and stood before her bare-chested.

"So are you," she said.

He gave a short laugh. "Somehow I never thought of myself that way."

"Maybe you should start." Daring greatly, she took a step closer to him. Never had she felt so vividly aware of the differences between a man and woman. His sheer size and ruggedness fascinated her. Hardly aware of what she was doing, she reached out and lightly touched his nipple.

He jerked and grabbed her hand with his. "Easy, sweetheart, at least if you want this to last."

Without giving her a chance to answer, he grabbed the hem of her dress in his big hands and balled it up until he could lift it over her head. Cool air touched her bare legs. It had been just warm enough to dispense with panty hose. Besides the bra, she wore only bikini panties.

Heat flushed her skin, following the path of his eyes as they moved over her. He sucked in his breath. His jaw flexed and for the first time she realized how hard he was fighting for control. The knowledge both thrilled and frightened her.

"It's okay," he said quickly as he caught the sudden tremor at the corner of her mouth. Huskily he added, "I'd never do anything to hurt you, Lisa. I swear it."

She believed him. If he had been capable of forcing a woman, he would not be standing there before her, giving her the time she needed. He wasn't a man who thought only of his own desires.

Even so, he took a deep shuddering breath before he said, "We'll go as slowly as you want, I promise."

"No," Lisa said softly.

He flinched. "What's that?"

"No," she repeated, and stepped closer so that her breasts brushed the rough hair of his chest. Head raised, she met his eyes bravely. "I don't want to go slowly, Mark." Her voice faltered before a sudden wave of heat but she persisted. "I need you so much I can't wait."

He looked at her, stunned for just a moment before something seemed to snap deep inside him.

"Sweet heaven, I hope you know what you're asking for."

Before she could answer, his arms closed around her, dragging her against his granite-hard length. Without hesitation, his mouth took hers, his tongue plunging wildly. Through the rough fabric of his jeans, his erection pressed against her smooth skin.

She hardly knew when he tipped them both back onto the bed. The sheets were cool against her heated body. He undid the front clasp of her bra and lifting her slightly, stripped it off.

With both his hands, he covered her breasts, kneading them gently. His palms were callused. The slight abrasiveness increased the sensualness of the caress almost unbearably.

Her head tossed back and forth against the pillows. She tried to say his name but his tongue was in her mouth again, thrusting in and out even as he slipped his fingers into her panties.

His touch there was infinitely gentle. Slowly, he parted and stroked her, murmuring thick sounds of encouragement deep in his throat.

Consciousness faded. There was nothing now except this man and the exquisite tension he built within her. The world whirled down to a tiny vortex of pleasure growing tighter and tighter until suddenly it exploded.

Her back arched. She clung to his, digging her fingers into his muscled shoulders.

Dimly, she was aware of him pulling off her panties. His hands skimmed her thighs, stroking the sensitive inner flesh.

She opened her eyes, dazed. He loomed above her, big and hard, all male strength and demand.

Yet, still he waited until she slipped a hand down between their bodies and found him. He moaned thickly as she guided them together.

The sheer size of him took her breath away and she faltered for a moment, but already the driving, surging need was tightening in her again.

"Please," she whispered, "now."

His arms, corded with muscle and sinew, were braced on either side of her. Holding his weight off, he moved hard and fast. She cried out and raised her hips, drawing him even further into her.

They moved together, locked in an ancient rhythm, bodies glistening. Pleasure mounted, growing higher and hotter, until the moist inner folds of her body convulsed around him, taking them both to shattering release.

Chapter 18

There was just no way to ask her delicately, Mark decided. If he wanted an answer to the question that had been going around and around in his mind ever since he woke up, he was going to have to be direct.

It was deep in the quiet of the night. He had woken from sleep so profound that he felt as though he hadn't moved a muscle since consciousness had slipped from him. Certainly he had not dreamt, for he woke with his mind fully clear, undimmed by phantom images and almost painfully alert.

She was there, standing by the window with her back to him. Naked she stood, slender and pale, staring out at the night. Her arms were wrapped around her. He wondered if she were cold.

Slowly he straightened against the pillows. His body felt strangely heavy, as though it resented being asked to move. So complete had his satiation been that merely to stir seemed an unkindness.

Yet he sat up, the sheet falling to his hips, and looked at her. Sweet heaven, she was beautiful. Not merely the seductive shape of her body but far more.

Here, in the dark and quiet, there seemed to be a luminous light within her that he felt obscurely privileged to glimpse. A tiny kernel of embarrassment moved in him, astounding considering how intimately he had possessed her and she him. Yet he understood it, for he felt as if he were looking at her very soul.

Still, he had to know.

The silence ruptured when he cleared his throat. She turned slowly, gazing at him over her shoulder. "You're awake," she said.

He smiled faintly. "I'm a little surprised myself."

She made no attempt to cover her nakedness but instead let her arms drop and stared at him as fully as he studied her. "I hope I didn't disturb you."

"Oh, but you did. Enormously."

She laughed at that, a high, free sound that curled through him like sunshine breaking through clouds. "Did I?" she murmured.

"Yes, indeed, Miss Lisa Morley. I'm a shaken man."

"You look," she said, "like a wicked one."

It was his turn to laugh for she said it most deliciously, as though calling his bluff.

He held out a hand. "Not wicked. Lonely."

She sighed, exaggeratedly, and he held his breath, waiting to see what she would do. Her head tilted to one side.

She took one step, and then another, moving with exquisite grace of which he knew she wasn't remotely conscious. Her head was back, her carriage proud. She challenged him with every breath, tempted him by merely being.

His hand reached out, catching hers. She dug her heels into the thick carpet and resisted. With a fraction of his strength, carefully measured out, he dragged her onto the bed and in an instant had her under him.

"Wicked, is it?" he asked.

"A terrible man."

He smiled, teeth gleaming white against the whiskered shadows of his jaw, and shifted slightly so that he lay within her warm, parted thighs.

"All wrong for you," he said, his tone half teasing and yet carrying the buried vulnerability he'd felt so keenly hours before.

She touched a finger to his mouth, tracing the hard, chiseled lips. Her breathing quickened. "I wouldn't say that."

He shut his eyes for a moment, unwilling to reveal what he sensed must be in them. Instead he caught her finger between his teeth, biting lightly and was rewarded by a soft moan.

Against his manhood, he felt her growing hot and damp, ready for him. His response was immediate and unmistakable. Her eyes widened, making him grin.

"Not too long ago, I was thinking that I felt sixteen again."

Passion danced behind the green and gold veils of her soul. "If this is what you were like then, no wonder I was scared of you."

"Were you really?" he asked, surprised. She had always seemed so cool and collected, even as a very young girl.

When all the rest of them were going through adolescent hell, Lisa Morley had glided through life, every hair in place, skin perfect, straight *A's* and a ready smile. Scared?

"You were everything I wasn't ready to deal with," she said. "Dangerous, exciting. When I looked at you, I felt as though I was seeing the whole wide world beyond the safe little place I knew."

"That's funny. When I looked at you, I thought I was getting a glimpse of heaven."

Her smile faltered. Softly she said, "If I'd known..."

"You would have run like crazy and you'd have been right. I was still hurting too bad back then."

"And now...?"

"Now..." He gritted his teeth as waves of pleasure moved through him. He wasn't even in her yet and still the passion was almost more than he could bear.

"It's not exactly pain I'm feeling."

She threaded her fingers in his hair, stroking down the hard column of his neck. Huskily she murmured, "I'm glad."

He inhaled sharply, determined to hold onto his control if only a few moments longer. "There's something I want to know."

"Right now?"

"Hmm...I think so." Staring down into her eyes, he thought about all she had been through, this proud, strong woman who had only to touch him with her eyes to make him hard as a randy boy.

"About Chas," he murmured against the sweet, smooth skin of her throat. "I know he's Jimmy's dad, but is there ... uh ... something wrong with him?"

She stiffened slightly. "Wrong?"

"Yeah, wrong. I mean, the way you tell it, he walked out on you because you got pregnant with his child."

"Ran would be closer to the truth."

He raised himself slightly so that they were touching only below the waist. Her eyes were wide, her lips full and parted.

There were slight abrasion marks on her breasts from their earlier lovemaking. He was sorry for them even as he felt a spurt of primitive gladness that she bore his mark. Holding his weight on one arm, he reached out and covered her breast, stroking the hard nipple with his thumb. She bit her lip, trying to hold back a moan.

"You're the sexiest woman I've ever known," he said bluntly. It was the truth. He was only just beginning to realize that what he'd experienced with her— and was experiencing right now—went far beyond anything he'd ever known.

A few short weeks before, he would have said that sex held no more surprises for him. But that was before the rain-swept night on the road outside of town. Before finding Lisa again. Now he knew he would have been wrong.

Her lashes fell, hiding her thoughts. There was an edge to her voice as she asked, "Are you fishing for compliments?"

He frowned. "What do you mean?"

"Just what I said. Are you?"

"No, of course not. What's that got to do with—"
He stopped, studying her intently. Slowly a smile of
pure masculine satisfaction spread across his face.
"You mean..."

"Darn you, Mark Fletcher, you know perfectly well
what I'm saying."

"No, I don't."

"I'm not spelling it out."

He touched her with his knee, nudging her thighs
farther apart and in the process making her unmistakably aware of the extent of his arousal. "Want to
bet?"

"You're insufferable." The slumberous heaviness of
her eyelids belied her words.

"Let's see now, wicked, terrible *and* insufferable.
What's next?"

"What I said before, dangerous."

"And exciting, you said that, too."

"Is there anything worse than a man who will throw
a woman's words up to her?"

"Yes," he said, suddenly serious. "A man who isn't
there when he ought to be."

He felt the breath go out of her and for a moment
hated himself for dredging up such painful memories. But he truly had to know. More important, he
wanted to make sure she knew what was happening
between them.

He doubted she realized that her hands had been
stroking his back, or that they stopped now and
pressed into his hard flesh, as though she was seeking
something to hold onto.

The words were dragged from her. "Chas...was
fun. He was daring, glamorous, unexpected. He

turned my world upside down and for a while I liked it that way."

She paused, but then went on, more willingly. "Maybe it didn't seem that way to you, but I was something of a grind even when we were in high school. That didn't change once I started working. If anything, it got worse until Chas came along."

"He made you see that life was more than work?"

"You could say that. He could be absurdly impulsive and wholeheartedly generous. There was a very endearing quality to him. At the time, I didn't realize..."

"What?"

"I don't know exactly. In some ways, he'd never grown up. What I never figured out was why."

"Maybe being filthy rich and spoiled rotten had something to do with it."

"Maybe, but through him, I met other people in similar positions. Some I liked, some I didn't. Chas was different."

Mark was starting to regret bringing the subject up in the first place. There was a hint of tenderness in her voice, almost as though she didn't completely blame the bastard for what he'd done.

"That's one way to put it," he said. "Abandoning a wife and child is different, all right."

"Actually, it happens all the time. Chas was being completely consistent with what passes for morals these days."

"That's crap and you know it. Plenty of men would tear out their hearts rather than desert their families."

She blinked, as though shaking off memory. Her hands softened, no longer clinging to him but moving with feather lightness down his back to his narrow hips. There she clasped him, her fingers pressing against his buttocks as her body lifted against his intimately.

"Do you really want to keep talking about Chas?"

"No," he said, his throat constricted. Color stained his high cheekbones. He didn't want to talk about anything. Or think or remember or question.

All he wanted was to be moving deep inside her, listening to the little raw sounds coming from her throat and feeling the walls of her body undulate around him.

Besides that, nothing else counted. He wouldn't let it.

Almost roughly, he gathered her to him. Dimly, he knew he had to go slowly, not risk hurting her. But she was already more than ready for him. He groaned with relief even as her hand closed around him, drawing him into silken heat.

Much later Lisa lay, not yet asleep, not yet awake, either, drifting in a sort of half consciousness. Mark was beside her. She could feel the warmth of his body and hear the regular rise and fall of his breath.

Her body was so completely sated that it seemed to float in some state of being from which all need had been banished, at least temporarily. But such was not the case with her mind. It remained sharply aware.

He'd been right, of course, when he'd guessed that this was not how it had been between her and Chas.

Their early months together had been good, she couldn't deny that. But never, never like this.

There had never been anything remotely like this, at least not for her. With Mark, she seemed utterly unable to hold anything back. He possessed her so completely, whether he knew it or not, that it terrified her to think of it. With him, she forgot everything, all doubt and caution, all modesty, everything. He left no part of her untouched.

She turned her head, gazing at him. Even asleep, he looked like exactly what he was, a tough, hard man who met life on his own terms. In the pale light, she could make out the thin white scars on his arms and chest where he had been injured.

There were other wounds, as well, unseen yet all the more potent. He was a survivor who didn't hesitate to take whatever he decided he wanted.

She should be as afraid of him as she had been at sixteen, maybe more. Instead, she loved him.

The knowledge of that came to her simply, slipping into her thoughts as easily as a long-expected friend. Yet one who came in a guise she would never have anticipated.

Or would she? Was grown-up Lisa Morley truly all that different from the girl-woman yearning to reach out to the wild boy who even then touched her more deeply than anyone else could?

She would never know. The past was done, the future elusive. There was only now, these hours, these days, stolen from a world that could intrude without warning.

Sighing, she snuggled more closely against his warmth and strength. He murmured something and slipped an arm around her waist, drawing her into the protective curve of his body.

Her eyes closed. Presently, she slept.

Chapter 19

Mark was gone when she woke again. The pillow beside her still bore the imprint of his head and the sheets retained his heat. She turned over, nuzzling her face into the pillow, breathing in the musky perfume of passion.

It was still very early. He couldn't have gone far. She started to leave the bed but stopped suddenly, reconsidering. Unaccustomed shyness seized her. After what they had shared the night before, and what she had realized about her feelings, she wasn't sure she was ready to confront him just yet. She needed time to rebuild her defenses, at least a little.

Still, if Jimmy wasn't already up, he would be soon. She didn't want him to come looking for her and find her in Mark's bed. Quickly she rose and padded into the bathroom.

A steaming hot shower helped restore her equanimity or what passed for it. Wrapped in a huge white terry-cloth robe she found hanging on the door, she slipped down the hall.

A swift glance in Jimmy's room showed his small form still snuggled under the covers. She left him there and went on. Her own bed gave clear testament to the fact that she had spent the night elsewhere. It remained perfectly made, just as she had left it the previous day.

She hung the robe away in the closet, intending to return it later, and dressed. The short russet leather skirt and white silk blouse she put on might not look much like armor, but they made her feel considerably better equipped to confront whatever might lie ahead.

First, she had to make plans for Jimmy. It was great that Sam and the others had taken care of him the previous day, but she didn't feel right about continuing to impose on them. Neither did she feel safe enough to take him back to Nancy MacEnroe's.

She had two phone calls to make and she did them in quick succession. Jane answered on the first ring, almost as though she'd been waiting.

"You have reached the residence of Jane MacEnroe. She is not here. At the sound of the beep, please leave a message. Beep."

"Idiot," Lisa said fondly. "It's me."

"No kidding? Where are you?"

Lisa's stomach fell. She had presumed her friend knew where she was. If she'd been wrong, Jane must have been worried. And she'd have every reason to be angry.

"I thought your mom would have told you, I'm at Mark's."

"Still?"

Relieved that her whereabouts hadn't been a total mystery, Lisa said, "Yes, still."

"You're not as dumb as you were starting to act."

"Thanks," Lisa murmured. She wanted to get off the subject of Mark as quickly as she could. "Listen, I hate to ask you, but I really need a favor."

"Sure."

Warm gratitude spread through her. That was typical of Jane. In Lisa's opinion, there were basically two types of people in the world, the sures and the what-is-its. They revealed themselves the moment anyone asked for a favor.

Maybe the sures were a little naive and ran the risk of being exploited, but in Lisa's book nobody was better to have on her side. Jane was a sure-and-a-half.

"Is there any chance you could come out here for a little while today?" Jane was an artist and a successful one. She had what Lisa sometimes thought was the ultimate luxury, control over her own time. "I need to run some errands and I don't want to take Jimmy with me."

"Mainly because Mark would have a fit, right? He's not going to be too thrilled about you wandering around on your own, either."

"I'm a grown woman," Lisa said. After last night, he couldn't possibly have any doubt about that. "I'll go where I want to. But Jimmy really is better off here."

"I'm glad you realize that," Jane said. "I talked with Mom this morning. There's been no sign of those goons who were following you, but it's still better to be on the safe side. I'll be glad to come out. When do you want me?''

Lisa's shoulders sagged slightly. She hadn't realized how tense she was until just then. What she had to do was important, but without Jane's help, she would have had to forget about it.

Her plan was to leave the ranch without being noticed. It would take some doing, but she was determined to pull it off. She didn't have much choice. There was no doubt in her mind that if any of Mark's men saw her leave, they would report it to him immediately. Much as she disliked the deception, she didn't see that she had any other choice.

Jane arrived less than an hour later, after Lisa had completed her second call. She still looked sleepy and disheveled.

Lisa felt a twinge of guilt. "I'm sorry I called you so early."

"It's okay. Every once in a while, I like to see what the world looks like before ten a.m."

Jane was a notorious night owl, chronically cranky in the mornings, but for the sake of her friend she was willing to fight her natural inclinations.

Jimmy gave her a bright smile from the breakfast table. She tousled his head as she took a quick look around.

"Where's Mark?"

"Working, I guess. He left before I got up." As she spoke, Lisa felt her cheeks warming. She turned away hastily and busied herself at the sink.

Jane chuckled softly, not fooled for a moment. She didn't say anything but she did start humming to herself.

Lisa shot her a censorious glance that was blithely ignored. Plopping down in the chair next to Jimmy, Jane asked, "So what do you want to do today, kid?"

He shrugged. "Have some fun."

"Sounds good to me. Ever been fishing?"

Jimmy shook his head. He looked at the tall, slender woman beside him with frank curiosity. "Do you know how?"

"Do I know how? Ask your mother who caught the biggest trout ever seen in these parts."

"Danny Shepherd," Lisa said. "It weighed over eight pounds and he was so proud of it he kept it around until it started to stink."

Jane rolled her eyes. "Not Danny Shepherd. For heaven's sake, don't you remember anything? What about the trout I caught the summer we were both thirteen, when we swiped a frying pan from your mom's kitchen and made a fire down by the lake? Ate the whole thing and nearly made ourselves sick in the process."

"Oh, *that* trout," Lisa said, grinning. "I guess that was pretty big." Her smile faded as she turned serious. "If you're going to take Jimmy fishing, you'll have to be careful."

"Ah, Mom," her son protested, "you can't get hurt fishing." He thought for a moment, his brow furrowing. "Unless you're the fish."

Lisa put the remains of the orange juice back in the refrigerator. Her eyes locked with Jane's. "Even so."

Her friend nodded. She understood full well what Lisa was saying. Jimmy didn't have to remain cooped up in the house, it would be cruel to try to make him. But wherever he went on the farm, a watchful eye should be kept for strangers.

"I'll take good care of him," Jane said softly.

Lisa shot her a grateful smile. "Okay, then, you two go catch a humongous fish and I'll be back as quick as I can."

"Are you sure you should go alone?" Jane asked quietly as she walked Lisa to the back door.

"I think it's best."

Lisa picked up the jacket and purse she had already set out. With a final glance at Jimmy, she murmured, "I really will be back soon. There's just a couple of things I need to do."

"I hope you're right. Taking care of Jimmy is fine, but I've got a feeling if Mark catches me here without you, there'll be hell to pay."

Lisa didn't disagree, there was no point. Instead she gave her friend a reassuring squeeze on the arm and opened the door. "Thanks for doing this. I really appreciate it."

"No trouble," Jane assured her. But her eyes were worried. She really didn't want to face Mark alone and Lisa didn't blame her.

Hurrying, she found Jane's car where her friend had left it, as requested, far enough away from the house not to be seen. The keys were still in it. She turned the engine on carefully, applied just a tiny amount of gas, and let the car coast.

Luck was with her for the road slanted downward. Not until she was well away from the farm did she gun the motor and really get moving.

Jane would take Jimmy fishing. If anyone saw them, it would be easy to explain. A friend of his mother's dropping by to keep them company. Sam and the others certainly knew Jane and had no reason to doubt her. They'd presume Lisa was back at the house.

So far, so good. Now all she had to do was get into town, take care of her "errands" and get back before Mark returned.

She drove quickly but carefully. The last thing she wanted to do was risk getting a speeding ticket from one of Sheriff Nagel's loyal deputies. Nagel himself would no doubt report back to Mark as quickly as any of the farmhands would have.

The need to restrain her natural impulse and not hurry too much did nothing for her nerves. By the time she finally pulled up in front of her house, her heart was pounding and she had a sick feeling deep in her stomach.

Nonetheless, she got out immediately and went around to the back door. Her second phone call this morning, to Fred Baker, had confirmed that the things she'd asked for from her apartment had been sent on. They should have arrived the previous day.

Langston being the small town that it was, when the postman had found no one at home, he'd simply left the boxes on the back porch where he figured they'd be safe enough. He'd been right. They appeared to have been undisturbed.

Quickly, Lisa carried them inside and set them on the kitchen table. There were four in all, mostly filled with her own belongings since almost everything of Jimmy's had been brought in the car. She welcomed the chance to expand her wardrobe, but she was more interested in several particular items she'd asked the superintendent to include.

They were right on top of the first box she opened. Her hand shook slightly as she lifted the framed photo and the small, leather-bound book. The photo was of Chas, taken shortly after they were married. She had kept it strictly for Jimmy's sake.

Not that he'd shown much interest. After glancing at it once or twice, he'd ignored it. Eventually she'd put it away again. More than a year had passed since she'd last looked at it.

Her first impression was that Chas was as handsome as she remembered him, with the rugged good looks and endearing smile that seemed to promise a wonderful time. But hard on that came the realization that she could stare at his picture without feeling much of anything.

Certainly, she felt no pain or longing, no desperate surge of unrequited love. He was simply a good-looking man she'd known and for whom she still had vague affection.

But that was absurd. He was responsible for her being here. He had so frightened her that she'd fled hundreds of miles to be free of him. She'd even told him directly that if he came near her son, she would respond violently.

So how was it that she could look at his picture without experiencing the most intense loathing and fear?

Shaking her head at the peculiarity of her own nature, she put the photo aside temporarily and picked up the small black book. It had belonged to Chas. He'd left it behind when he'd departed four years ago and had never asked for it back. She'd forgotten it even existed until she'd spoken with Fred Baker and he'd offered to send belongings out to her.

Her hands brushed the smooth leather binding. Although she'd never given the book much importance, she had taken a quick look inside when she'd first come across it.

The book was arranged alphabetically with dozens of names, addresses and phone numbers penciled in. But in addition there were also scribbled notes about appointments and other reminders Chas had written to himself. She supposed it was the closest he might ever have come to having a diary.

It had never occurred to her that the book might contain information she could use. It still didn't. But she was worried and desperate enough to consider any possibility. Before she was done, she resolved to look through every single page of the thing even if she ended up learning nothing at all.

That would have to wait. A quick glance at the kitchen clock told her she had already been away from the farm an hour. Quickly she selected the clothes she wanted and piled them on the table along with the photo of Chas and his address book.

Upstairs, the house was cool and quiet. A floor-board creaking under her foot made her jump. She took a deep breath to calm herself and kept going.

Five minutes later she was back downstairs with the pile of belongings in her arms. Locking the door behind her, she walked quickly to the car. Her purse hung heavily over her shoulder. Inside, the gun shifted slightly, bouncing against her hip.

Jane and Jimmy were at the stream behind the house when she got back. Her son saw her first and jumped up, running toward her with a beaming smile.

"We did it, Mommy! We caught a fish!" He couldn't have been more proud if he'd landed a hundred of them. Lisa laughed and gave him a quick hug.

"Good for you. Did you thank Jane for teaching you?"

"He did indeed," Jane said as she stood up. She shot her friend a questioning glance. "Everything go all right?"

"Just fine. Any problems?"

Jane correctly took that to mean had any of the men come sniffing around. She shook her head. "It's been quiet."

"Good. I don't know if Mark is planning to be back for lunch but you'd certainly be welcome to stay."

"Some other time," Jane said with a grin. Under her breath, she added, "I don't want to wear out my welcome."

Lisa laughed and handed over the keys to her car. "Thanks again," she said genuinely. "You really came through."

Jane shrugged. "What are friends for?" She turned to go, thought better of it, and looked at Lisa over her shoulder. "You'll be careful, right?"

"I am being careful, that's why I'm here."

"I know, but I thought..."

"What?"

"That you were going to let Mark handle this. When you saw the light and accepted his invitation, I figured that was what it meant."

Slowly Lisa said, "I really appreciate what Mark's doing, but I can't just turn everything over to him. Jimmy is my child. Ultimately, *I'm* the one who's responsible."

Jane couldn't argue with that and she didn't try. But she did go away looking worried.

Chapter 20

Mark didn't return to the house for lunch. He stayed out in the fields checking the irrigation system and made do with a sandwich he'd brought along.

He told himself it was because he had a lot of work to do. It was almost time for planting and he wanted to make sure everything went smoothly. Besides, he was getting a little worried about the weather.

The real truth was he wasn't sure what would happen when he saw Lisa again. Before that happened, he wanted to at least take the edge off. If he could wear himself out first, maybe he could go home and act like a civilized human being instead of hauling her under him the minute he set eyes on her.

On the other hand, he thought with a grin, civilization was overrated. Lisa Morley was some kind of woman. Whatever old Chas had been, real smart wasn't part of the package. No man who walked out on a living, breathing dream could claim to be anything but hangdog dumb.

The question was, was he dumb enough to be causing all the trouble? Like it or not, Mark couldn't shake the feeling that the answer he wanted didn't add up.

As far as he saw it, Lisa's ex had been okay until he found out they had a kid coming. Then he hightailed it, never to be seen again. But he made sure she got a support check every month, when a lot of men, including men with money, couldn't be bothered. How come?

There was more. Lisa suspected Chas was behind what had been happening, but she didn't really believe it. She couldn't have and still sound the way she did when she mentioned his name.

At least she didn't come across as still being in love with him. The hot, sweet response of her body the previous night had put that fear to rest. But she didn't hate Chas the way she could be expected to if he was really what was threatening Jimmy.

That seemed to puzzle her, too. She was trying to figure it out the same way Mark was. He wondered if she was having any better luck.

Finally it got to the point where he couldn't find any more reason for staying out. The light was starting to fade, clouds were rolling in from the west and the breeze had taken on an edge.

On impulse, he'd left the pickup behind and taken his favorite horse instead. The gray stallion stood patiently waiting for him as he finished checking the last valve on the length of pipe that ran into the south fields.

Mark patted the horse's neck gently as he mounted. With a last look out over his land, he satisfied himself that everything was as it should be. Feeling a good kind of tired, he turned toward home.

Despite the clouds, the western horizon was still clear enough for a magnificent sunset. Streaks of violet, amber and pale green melted into fiery orange. Except for the sky, color was slowly bleaching out of the world, being replaced by the muted gray of twilight.

Mark crested the top of the last hill before the farmhouse and stopped for a moment, looking down over the sloping lawns. The lights were on, beacons of gold against the coming dark. He could make out a twisting wisp of smoke rising from the chimney.

Digging his heels lightly into the gelding, he urged the horse on.

Lisa stood on the porch, still wearing the russet leather skirt and white silk blouse she had put on that morning. The clothes weren't really warm enough now but she was too distracted to notice.

As the day wore on, Mark occupied more and more of her thoughts. She kept wondering where he was and what he was doing. When it began to get late and he still hadn't returned, she even began to worry about him.

The sun was going down in glory. She watched it for a while, studying the palette of colors spread out across the sky. The city had cut her off from nature. She had lost track of the subtler rhythms of the days giving way one to another, the seasons passing with their eternal promise of renewal. There had been only hot and cold, wet and dry, scrambling from home to office, darting into the subway, darting back out, always hurrying to the next chore, the next responsibility.

Not here. Here she had time to stand on a porch and watch night gently embrace the world. Time, too, to think of the man who had possessed her with such thirsting passion and in the process been possessed himself.

Her body stirred longingly at the mere thought of him. Despite the growing chill, she felt warmed from within. Her nipples poked against the silk blouse. She shivered slightly and turned to go back inside.

From the corner of her eye she saw the rider. He had appeared suddenly on the crest of the hill, silhouetted there against the darkening sky.

As she stared at him, she had the uncanny sense that he was looking directly at her despite the distance between them, seeing her exactly as she was at that moment, filled with longing for him.

Although she couldn't see his face clearly, she didn't doubt for a moment that it was Mark. The powerfully masculine stance of his body atop the horse was achingly familiar to her. She felt almost as though she could reach out across the intruding space and touch him as easily as her lips now shaped his name.

As though in response, he urged the horse forward. Dust swirls rose from beneath the flashing hooves. Faster they came until she thought she could feel the pounding beats up through the ground and into her. Abruptly he drew rein in front of the porch. The horse reared slightly but settled quickly.

Crystalline-blue eyes swept over her, making her feel suddenly exposed. The chiseled lines of his face looked deeper than usual, as though carved into bronzed sinew and bone. The cambric work shirt he wore strained across his broad shoulders and chest. His sleeves were rolled up to the elbows, exposing burnished forearms rippling with muscle. Long, powerful legs encased in well-worn jeans gripped the horse's sides. He looked hard, dirty, infinitely male and utterly magnificent.

Lisa swallowed with difficulty. This man whose body had possessed hers with such fierce demand might almost have been a stranger, sitting up there on the proud horse, his gaze sharp-edged and unrelenting. There was no softness in him. Yet he was always gentle with Jimmy and even on occasion with herself. A man, then, of contradictions and mystery that she longed to solve.

Her head lifted. She caught the merest twitch at the corner of his mouth and smiled. "Dinner's almost ready."

He gave a short jerk of his head. "Good. Do I have time to get cleaned up?"

Deliberately, she ran her eyes over him, work-stained and dust-splattered as he was. "Looks like you'd better."

Mark pulled lightly on the reins. Without further urging, the horse turned toward the barn.

Lisa went back inside the house. She ignored the trembling that coursed through her and, with all the calmness she could muster, began setting the table.

* * *

Sam was still working in the horse barn. He came out as Mark rode up on the gray and dismounted.

"Everything quiet?" Mark asked.

Sam nodded. "Seems so." He cocked his head toward the house. "Friend of hers came over, Jane MacEnroe. Took the boy fishing. Looked like he did okay."

"That's good," Mark said absently. He appreciated Sam's reassurance, but at the moment all he could think of was Lisa. The bright warmth of the house reached out to him, drawing him irresistibly.

She was in the kitchen. Jimmy was with her. They had their heads bent together and were laughing softly.

He left them to it and headed for the shower. Briefly he glanced at his bed as he passed. When he left that morning, it had been warm, rumpled and filled with satisfied woman.

Now it was neatly made, the sheets smoothed and the quilt back in place. As he undid the buttons of his shirt, he picked up a corner of the quilt and took a quick look under it. Fresh sheets had been put on. A slow smile curved his mouth.

In the bathroom, he tossed his clothes in the hamper as he waited for the water to heat up. When steam misted the mirror, he stepped into the shower. The shock felt good against his skin. A day's worth of weariness sloughed off along with the inevitable dirt and grime.

Absently he lathered the soap over his chest and arms. The water darkened his body hair, trailing down his washboard-flat abdomen to the thick thatch at his groin. Muscles bunched in his powerful thighs and calves. He tossed his head back, sending gleaming droplets of water in all directions, and reached for the shampoo.

Five minutes later he stepped out of the shower and toweled himself dry. Running a hand over his jaw, he decided on a quick shave. That done, he dressed in fresh jeans and a shirt. By the time he returned to the kitchen, good smells filled the air.

Jimmy launched himself at him. Mark laughed and scooped him up. They roughhoused for several minutes, Mark carefully gentle, until Lisa called a halt.

With an indulgent smile, she said, "Time out. Jimmy, go wash your hands. Dinner's going on the table."

He ran off, leaving them momentarily alone. Lisa shot him a quick glance but then looked away. Her cheeks were warm.

As she walked toward the big oak table, he stepped in front of her and reached for the plates she was carrying. "Here, let me."

She looked up through the thick fringe of her lashes. Their eyes met. Mark's body tightened. He had the sudden, shocking sensation that he was falling, tumbling over himself and into a green and gold glade where the haunting music of heartbeats played and there was no reality beyond the one they created.

With an effort, he caught himself. His breath was ragged and he felt washed by heat from within. Lisa took a quick step backward. She looked as startled as he felt.

Mark only just managed not to drop the plates. He set them out on the table, added the cutlery and even remembered the napkins, but he did it all with no conscious thought whatsoever. When Jimmy came back and filled the room with his bright chatter, Mark was grateful for it. The child was a welcome distraction from the shimmering heat that flowed between the adults.

With pride Jimmy recounted how he'd caught the fish they were having for dinner. Mark praised him and promised to take him fishing again. They went on to the subject of ponies, with Lisa cautiously giving her permission for Jimmy to start learning how to ride.

The child's innocent happiness and sheer, unbridled pleasure helped to ease the tension that would otherwise have been unbearable. But when dinner was over and the clearing up done, the tension returned.

Mark couldn't look at Lisa without wanting to touch her. When she brushed past him at the sink, he had to clench his hands to keep from reaching for her. She saw it and paused, eyes wide, before quickly moving away.

Jimmy came to the rescue again, asking Mark to read him a bedtime story.

"Do you mind?" Mark asked Lisa.

She shook her head, not meeting his eyes. "Not if you don't. Go ahead, I'll finish up here."

He went down the hall with the child's hand clasped trustingly in his own and the soft clatter of the dishes fading behind them.

Chapter 21

"Would you like a drink?" Mark asked. He had returned to the great room after tucking Jimmy in. The little boy had fallen asleep while they were reading stories.

Looking down at his small head nestled against the pillows, Mark had known a surge of protectiveness not unlike what he experienced with Lisa. Hard on it came further thoughts of Jimmy's biological father, none of them flattering.

For one of the very few times since he quit, he almost regretted having given up alcohol. This was an occasion when he would have appreciated the mellowness a little of it could provide. However, club soda would still do fine.

"Whatever you're having," Lisa said. She was standing by the windows. He could see her reflection in the glass, etched against the velvety night. She was

so beautiful that she made him ache, but he realized
that his response to her went far beyond the physical.

Her spirit—her warmth and courage, her vitality
and strength—made him feel more alive than he had
in a very long time. Perhaps more than ever.

He brought her the drink and stood, close but not
touching. The scent of her perfume tantalized him. He
took a quick sip from his own glass and cast around
for a distraction.

"The weather's changing."

"Is it?"

He nodded. "Turning colder. Spring started a little
early. Seems like it was false."

"A false spring," Lisa mused. "There's something
rather sad about that."

His hand tightened on the glass. The sound of her
soft, feminine voice was like a caress running over his
entire body. The results were predictable.

He smiled ruefully. There were people—women for
the most part—who would find his uncharacteristic
vulerability nothing less than hilarious. After strut-
ting through all those years enjoying himself, he had
at last been brought low not by the disaster of his
marriage, which he had sloughed off, but by a decep-
tively delicate woman with steel in her spine.

Of all the opponents he'd met, she was in many
ways the most dangerous. What slashing blades and
slamming sticks hadn't been able to do, a mere whisper from Lisa Morley could accomplish without the
slightest difficulty.

He took another sip of the club soda but hardly
tasted it. The room was very quiet. Far in the background, he could hear a clock ticking. The sound

seemed to reverberate through him, reminding him of how inexorably time passed. Once gone, it could never be recaptured.

He set the glass down on a nearby table. His hand brushed across her shoulder, feather-light down the length of her arm, to close around her hand.

A small tremor ran through her. He felt it and smiled. Holding her eyes with his, he took her own glass and set it aside. "Are you very tired?"

She gave one quick shake of her head. "No, you?"

As an answer, he drew her to him, catching her hand between their bodies. His steely arm wrapped around her back. "All of a sudden, I've got tons of energy."

She laughed and raised her eyes boldly. Whatever doubts might have lingered in the green-gold shadows, he couldn't see them. There was only the sweet, beckoning curve of her mouth and the silken slide of her arms around his neck.

He gave a low groan. Molten heat surged through him. Desperately he struggled for control. He wanted to go slow, to savor every moment, but with her that seemed to be impossible.

As though sensing the struggle within him, Lisa moved her hips, only slightly but enough to send a jolt of almost painful arousal through him. He had no idea whether she acted unconsciously or not, and he didn't care. All thought vanished before the single, driving need to possess her.

Urgently, he pressed her against the wall beside the windows. Her head fell back as her fingers dug into the soft fabric of his shirt. A moment longer he hesitated, no more. The slumberous light in her eyes was all the further encouragement he needed.

Without preliminaries, he stabbed his tongue deep into her mouth. She cried out softly and pressed closer, clinging to him as he stroked her moist sweetness. He groaned again and tore his mouth away, raking his teeth down her exposed throat. His big, callused hands closed over her breasts, squeezing lightly.

Passion rocked them both. He could feel her nipples pressing through the thin fabric and hear the little whimpering sounds she made. A red mist swirled before his eyes. It was all he could do not to pull her down on the floor under him right then and there.

She deserved better than that. He had better give it to her while he still could. Bending slightly, he lifted her and strode swiftly down the hall. Her weight was slight in his powerful arms. Holding her, he strode quickly down the hall.

The bedroom was dark except for the light he'd left on in the adjoining bathroom. His hands shook slightly as he laid her on the bed. Swiftly, he moved away and stripped off his clothes, tossing them on the floor.

Lisa's eyes were smoky as he walked back toward her, unabashed in his nakedness. He enjoyed the way she looked at him, half cautious but fascinated all the same. The sensation was familiar to him. He felt it every time he looked at her.

Her gaze lingered on his aroused manhood. He watched the color seep across her cheeks and took several deep breaths, summoning what little was left of his control.

When she began to sit up, he pushed her gently back against the pillows. "Let me." Even to his ears, his voice sounded strained, as though it came from somewhere deep and dark.

She lay back, quiescent under him, but he could feel the rapid-fire beat of her heart. Fighting to ignore the urges crashing through him, he slowly undid the buttons of her blouse one after another. They were absurdly small and delicate. He could have crushed them beneath his fingers or simply ripped the fragile fabric apart. But he was determined to do this right.

When her blouse was open, he pulled it from beneath her waistband and with a hand beneath her back, slid it from her. In the shadowed light her skin looked like alabaster, the tips of her breasts touched by circles of budding rose.

His breathing was harsh. More quickly now, for his control was slipping, he lowered the zipper of her skirt and slipped that garment from her. Her panty hose were next. He peeled them off, one leg at a time, sliding each down her perfectly shaped thighs and calves, and over her pink-tinged toes.

He sat back then and studied his handiwork. She lay before him wearing only the tiny scraps of her bra and panties. Her skin was flushed, her lips parted and her eyes slumberous with need.

"Have you any idea," he asked hoarsely, "what I see when I look at you like this?"

Slowly, she shook her head.

The back of his fingers grazed her abdomen, circling the indentation of her navel. He lowered himself beside her, his hand drifting lower to stroke her inner thighs.

"Perfection," he murmured. "As magnificent as any statue, yet also magnificently alive. Warm... responsive..." His hand delved further, moving beneath her panties. "Welcoming..."

Her entire body clenched with the force of the pleasure she was experiencing. She raised her arms, trying to draw him to her, but he caught both her wrists in one hand and stretched them taut above her head.

"Not yet," he rasped, holding her. Through the thin lace, his tongue traced the shape of first one nipple and then the other. She cried out softly and struggled to free herself but he wouldn't allow it. Instead, he flicked the front closure of her bra open, baring her fully to his touch.

Lisa moaned helplessly as his mouth closed on her, suckling urgently, drawing her deeper and deeper even as his tongue continued to torment her swollen nipples. Her hips arched as her legs fell open.

"*Damn you,*" she cried out, "I can't stand this any more."

A purely male smile of satisfaction curved his hard mouth but with it came intense relief. He couldn't have held back a moment longer. Almost roughly, he pulled her panties off, spread her legs and moved between them.

Swiftly, he opened her with his fingers, making absolutely sure that she was ready for him before he plunged, hard and fast. She cried out again, lifting to meet each thrust.

She asked for no quarter and he offered none. Relentlessly he drove into her again and again. Her release came quickly and so powerfully that it pushed him, too, over the edge. The world shattered as he poured himself into her, life to life, whirling in a vortex where they were both truly one.

Chapter 22

Deep in the night, Mark awoke. He slipped from sleep to full alertness with no transition at all. One moment he was dreaming, the next he was wide awake and half rising, braced on his elbow.

Lisa was sitting on the other side of the room at a small desk. She was wrapped in his white terry-cloth robe. Her head was bent. She appeared to be studying something within the circle of light cast by the lamp.

As he watched, she sighed wearily and ran her fingers through her hair.

He rose, his feet soundless on the thick carpet, and walked toward her. So lost was she in whatever she was reading that she had no awareness of his approach until he touched her shoulder.

She jumped and whirled around. "What...!"

"Easy," he said. "I woke up and saw you sitting here. What's so fascinating?"

Lisa hesitated. Her hand crept as if to cover the book she'd been studying. But she thought better of it and shrugged.

"Nothing really. It's an old address book of Chas's. I remembered it was one of the few things he left behind and I thought I'd take a look through it on the off chance there might be something useful."

Mark frowned. He had decidedly mixed feelings about her leaving his bed to wander down memory lane with old Chas. But he couldn't really blame her for grasping at any chance to figure out what was really happening.

"Any luck?"

She shook her head. "As nearly as I can see, he was using this book the year we were married. I recognize some of the names, although certainly not all. There are also some notes scrawled in the back, appointments, things he needed to do, stuff like that."

"Any mention of needing to turn into a decent human being?"

She shot him a chiding glance. "Fat chance. However..." Her voice trailed off. She looked down at the book pensively.

Mark lifted it from the table and flipped through the pages. He was careless in his nudity, but out of the corner of his eye, he took note that Lisa wasn't quite so immune. Her cheeks warmed and her mouth, swollen from his kisses, parted slightly.

His mood improved. He handed the book back to her after a cursory glance. "However what?"

"There is some mention in here of a doctor Chas was apparently seeing. He noted regular appointments with him, sometimes as often as once a week if his schedule allowed but no less frequently than twice a month. The notes refer to a Dr. W., which wasn't much help except the addresses do include a Dr. David Walters with an office on Park Avenue."

"Did good old Chas have any medical problems? I mean, besides retarded personality development?"

Ignoring the gibe, Lisa shook her head. "Not that I ever knew of. He always seemed to be in excellent health and he certainly never mentioned going to see a doctor, let alone doing it regularly."

"Any idea what this Dr. Walters specializes in?"

"No, but it should be easy enough to find out. I'll call his office tomorrow."

"You're going to call and ask what kind of doctor he is? That'll sound a little strange."

"Do you have another suggestion?"

"Call the library. Ask a reference librarian to check the Manhattan Yellow Pages for you under physicians. They're usually grouped by specialty. If that doesn't work, call the American Medical Association. They might be more forthcoming."

Lisa nodded slowly. "You may be right. If there's anything to the mention of Walters, I don't want to make him suspicious."

"Then don't show your hand. Speaking of which..." He closed his fingers around hers and drew her gently out of the chair. "It's a very lovely hand, but I think it's looking lonely."

She laughed. "Do you really think so?"

"Oh, yes, that's definitely one lonely hand. Let's see the other."

Obligingly she gave it to him. "Yep, this one's lonely, too. How about the rest of you?" With a lecherous grin, he peered inside the oversized robe. "What do you know, a whole lonely body. We can't have that."

"You're crazy, you know that?"

"Must have been all those hockey pucks to the head."

Her eyes widened. "You're kidding, aren't you?"

He took one look at the genuine shock in her eyes and relented. "That crazy I wasn't. The helmet I wore could have taken a direct nuclear hit and kept on ticking."

Her instant relief moved him deeply. He liked the idea that she worried about him even as he moved quickly to assure her there was no need.

"Come back to bed."

She hesitated. "I guess I could use some sleep."

He smiled, drawing her against him. His breath was warm against her lips, his voice dark and deep. "Eventually."

"A psychiatrist?" Lisa repeated slowly. She shaped the word as though she had never said it before. As soon as she knew there would be someone at the main branch of the New York Public Library, she had called the reference desk.

The librarians there were famous for being able to put their fingers on the most obscure bits of information imaginable. Determining the specialty of one particular doctor out of the thousands practicing in the city was hardly a challenge.

"That's right," the man on the other end of the phone said. "Would you like his address and phone number?" he managed to ask without making it sound as though he thought she might be in need of the good doctor's services.

"No, thank you. I appreciate your help."

She hung up and stared at the opposite wall without seeing it. A psychiatrist. Chas had been seeing a psychiatrist on a regular basis through much—if not all—of their marriage and she hadn't known about it. Not only that, but she hadn't had the slightest clue.

It had never occurred to her that he had any emotional problems he could consider serious enough to seek help for, not until the very end, anyway, when he'd walked out because of her pregnancy. Sure, there'd been his reluctance to talk about his family, much less ever get her together with any of them, but he was hardly the first person to have difficulties in that area. She'd told herself that would all resolve itself eventually. It hadn't, and now she had to wonder what else she'd been wrong about.

She pressed her fingers to her mouth as dismay seeped over her. For the first time, she had to admit that she truly hadn't known Chas. In many ways—possibly crucial ones—he was a stranger to her. She had no real idea of what he was capable of.

Her hand was shaking, the fingers fluttering against her lips as though struck by an unseen wind. Abruptly she stood up and went to the kitchen door. Jimmy was playing right outside. She could see him clearly, hear his laugh as he ran with Bandit, feel the little-boy happiness he exuded.

Her son was safe, content, satisfied. She hadn't failed him, not ever. And she wasn't about to start now.

Before he went off that morning, Mark had cautioned her not to put too much store in anything the address book might reveal. The best protection, he insisted, was constant vigilance.

She had agreed, but she also knew that she couldn't go on like this forever. Inevitably, something would have to give.

She shut the door again and went back to the table. For several moments she stood beside it, staring down at the phone. The address book lay beside it but she didn't need to check for the number she wanted. Although she had never used it, she knew it by heart.

When Chas first left, she'd thought often about calling the number. Right after Jimmy was born, she had considered doing so again. Over the years, she'd thought less about it, but every once in a while it would flit through her memory, making her wonder if she was doing the right thing by keeping her distance.

Yet none of them had ever tried to get in touch with her. No one from Chas's family had ever called to find out if she was all right, if perhaps his child needed anything.

Their silence wasn't from ignorance. Chas had informed them of his marriage. She still remembered the letter his mother had written in response that so infuriated him he had thrown it into the fireplace and watched the heavy, cream-colored paper with its few sparse lines of meticulous script burn to ash.

Millicent Howell was a woman who could cut off her only son seemingly without a second thought simply because he'd made a marriage of which she did not approve. That hardly made Lisa want to know her. But Mother Howell—the mere thought of calling her that made Lisa's mouth twitch—just might hold the key to what had happened to Chas. And what might be happening with him now.

Gingerly, Lisa reached for the phone. She punched in the number before she could let herself think too much about what she was doing.

Chapter 23

Mark drew rein before the north fence that skirted the far side of the farm property. It was late morning. He had been at work since before dawn, leaving the warm, rumpled bed and the sleeping woman with palpable reluctance. But the day had beckoned and with it the weather that was beginning to worry him.

During the night it had turned sharply colder. He'd awakened to the sight of frost on the lawn beyond the house. Now astride his horse, he lifted the collar of his fleece-lined jacket and gazed out over the leaden sky.

Call it instinct, call it a guess. Call it anything anyone damn well pleased. He could swear he smelled snow.

His mouth tightened. What planting had already been started wouldn't be affected by snowfall. But the herd of sheep he also ran was a different matter. The lambs had begun to be born.

Grimly, he turned back toward the house. For once, he belatedly wished he'd brought the truck, but there was something about riding his own land that appealed to him too strongly to resist. The only problem was that it took him longer to get where he wanted to go.

By the time he dismounted, it was midmorning. Several of his men, Sam among them, were working around the barn. Jimmy was with them. He had already become a deft hand with a currycomb and showed no fear of the horses. Mark took note of that as he passed, reminding himself to start the boy riding soon.

Inside the house was quiet. He walked through the great room to the kitchen. Lisa was sitting at the table. She looked preoccupied.

"Something wrong?" he asked.

She glanced up, surprised to see him there. "I didn't hear you come in."

"You seemed pretty far away. What's going on?"

Lisa hesitated. Her slanting brows drew together. He had a sudden, almost overpowering impulse to smooth away the small furrow that appeared above her upturned nose.

"I'm not sure," she murmured.

He'd intended to be in and out quickly, to warn her that he suspected bad weather was coming and then be on his way. Instead he hooked a foot under one of the chairs, pulled it out and sat down. He left his jacket on but unbuttoned it and took off the heavy leather gloves he'd been wearing.

His gaze swept over her pale face, the hazel eyes dark with shadows. Anger stirred deep inside him.

Everything, all they had shared, and she still didn't trust him fully. A part of her remained aloof and sealed off. He couldn't completely blame her for that after what she'd been through, but it hurt all the same.

He ran a hand through his thick black hair and repressed an impatient sigh. There had been enough pain in his life. He wasn't anxious to open himself to more.

"Tell me what's bothering you." It wasn't a request and he didn't try to make it sound like one. She was living under his roof, under his protection. She had crept into his life and into his heart. She had made him confront feelings he hadn't believed he was capable of having.

She had filled him with joy. And she had made him hurt. He wasn't going to let her close him out now.

Her slender throat rippled as she swallowed nervously. Her eyelashes fluttered over her cheeks as she stared down at the hands she clasped so tightly.

"I called my mother-in-law."

Whatever he'd expected, it wasn't this. He leaned back in the chair and stared at her. "Who?"

"Ex-mother-in-law," she corrected. "Millicent Howell."

"Chas's mother?"

"That's right. Walters was—is—a psychiatrist. Chas saw him regularly for at least a year while we were married and I knew nothing about it. I thought maybe she could tell me why."

"And did she?"

"No, she didn't tell me anything at all. It was a very one-sided conversation."

''That surprises you? From what you've told me, it sounds like you always got the cold shoulder from the Howells.''

''I did, but there was more to it this time.'' She fell silent for a moment, trying to find the words to explain what bothered her. ''I wasn't surprised, but neither was she.''

''I don't follow.''

''This was the first time I'd ever spoken with her. She certainly knew I existed, but we'd never had any contact. Yet when I explained who I was, she didn't seem surprised at all to hear from me. It was almost as though she'd been expecting it.''

''You can't be sure of that.''

''No, I can't be, not a hundred percent at least. But that is the feeling I got. She asked no questions, not even how I'd gotten her number or found out about Walters. She refused to discuss him at all, although the way she did it, I'm not sure whether she knew about Chas going to see him or not. Basically, she refused to say anything.''

''Did you tell her you think Chas has been having you watched?''

''I said I wanted to get in touch with him and asked if she knew where he was.''

''And she said she didn't . . .''

Lisa shook her head. ''She didn't say one way or the other. 'I don't believe it would be appropriate.' That's what she said. She sounded . . . amused, almost.''

''Did you explain that it was important?''

''I said I was worried about Jimmy.''

''She knows who he is?''

"I don't know whether she does or not. She certainly didn't ask. She refused to be drawn out in any way." Lisa raised her eyes, meeting his. "I was her daughter-in-law. I'm her grandson's mother. We had never spoken before. Yet she had nothing she wanted to say to me or ask me. It was as though she already knew everything."

"But she couldn't, unless she's been in touch with Chas."

"Exactly."

Mark cursed under his breath. He didn't know whether Millicent Howell knew what her wayward son was up to or not. But he did know that the Howell family continued to obsess Lisa if only because of the danger she believed they posed to Jimmy. Until she was free of that, it couldn't be any different.

Belatedly she realized that his presence in the kitchen at that hour was unusual. "Is everything all right?" she asked.

"So far. I just came in to tell you the weather seems to be changing. We could be heading for some snow."

Lisa nodded. She'd lived in Langston long enough to be aware that snow even at this time of year wasn't unheard of. Instinctively she glanced out the window. Her frown deepened. "I didn't realize the clouds were so heavy."

"The forecast says chilly with a chance of showers, so maybe I'm wrong. But just in case . . ."

He didn't get any further. Lisa stood up at once and went over to the refrigerator, opening it. "We're a little low on supplies."

"We're very low," he corrected. A smile tugged at the corners of his mouth. "Shopping hasn't been my top priority."

"Well, it better be now. I'll make a list."

He nodded. Maybe she'd lived in town and gone away to the big city, but she had the instincts of a sensible farm girl. Bad weather could be coming. Better load up the larder.

"There's a lot I have to take care of around here," he said. "Would you mind getting whatever's needed?"

She shook her head, already busy scribbling. She looked a whole lot livelier than she had a few minutes before. He got the impression she didn't mind having something real and solid to deal with, something she could actually do something about.

"There's money in the drawer," he said, indicating which one. His gaze slipped to the windows and the sky again. "Get plenty."

"For the men, as well?"

He nodded. "They do their own cooking, but if we get a good blow, we'll be stuck for days."

"Is it all right if I take the truck?"

"Sure." He tossed her the keys. "You'll leave Jimmy here, right?"

She glanced up. "Of course I will, and Mark..."

"Yeah?"

"Thanks. I needed something to do."

He laughed, absurdly glad that he'd made her feel better even if he couldn't rightly take credit for it, and dropped a quick kiss on her upturned mouth. At least, it was supposed to be quick. Somehow, it didn't turn out that way.

By the time they drew apart, his voice was husky. "Don't thank me. It's Mother Nature who's looking to stir up trouble."

"Better her than Mother Howell," Lisa murmured, and went back to her list.

Chapter 24

Millicent Howell sat in her antique-filled, brocade-walled living room high above New York's Fifth Avenue. The windows were shut to block out the hum of traffic below. Soft, classical music played from hidden speakers.

The air was filtered and lightly scented with the peach and ginger potpourri she currently favored. Even the light passing through the silk draperies was subtly altered to meet her requirements. She liked things her own way.

For the first twenty-two years of her life, she had been forced to accept other people's notions of how she should behave. Primarily that had meant meeting the expectations of her wealthy parents and the society in which they moved.

Then she met David Winthrop Howell, fifteen years her senior, possessor of one of the oldest and most respected names in America, and, not incidentally, rich as Midas.

Her parents had been delighted by the marriage, which appeared to justify everything they believed about who they were and what they deserved. Howell himself had been pleased to acquire a perfectly trained wife and hostess that he presumed would meet all his requirements while leaving him free to indulge his less savory appetites elsewhere.

Millicent had walked down the aisle knowing she was walking to the only kind of freedom that mattered to her. The freedom that came from power and the will to use it ruthlessly.

As she had through almost four decades of supreme rule as the social leader of New York, not a small accomplishment considering that city still served as the financial hub for much of the world. Her rivals—when she deigned to even admit that she had any—had to be content with smaller provinces, Washington, D.C., for one, Atlanta, San Francisco. But New York was entirely hers.

She decided who mattered and who didn't. Politicians payed obeisance to her. Designers, decorators, artists and writers panted for her attention. Columnists sat at her feet and anyone, absolutely anyone, with aspirations to enter the city's social whirl, knew that success was impossible without her favor.

On more than one occasion she'd crushed a promising career simply to demonstrate that she could do it. On others, she had elevated a mediocrity to fame and fortune.

Power. She loved it and lived for it. Beside its seductive embrace, nothing mattered. Certainly not her husband, who had long since gone to his dubious reward, dead in the arms of a twin sister act. As for her sons, she preferred not to think of them at all, so gravely had they both disappointed her.

Poor, stupid Lisa Morley. The girl was getting what she deserved for having the effrontery to marry a Howell. It amused Millicent no end to think of how she must be squirming.

But not for much longer. Soon it would all be over. She would win again, as she always did.

She was not so naive as to think it would be easy. Chas had never properly accepted her authority no matter what lengths she went through to make him do so. No, he would refuse to give in. She would have to force him.

Yet, she had to be honest, if only with herself. That would make her victory all the sweeter.

She stood, a woman of medium height who appeared taller because of her extreme thinness. Impeccably dressed with every pale blond hair in place, she stepped in front of the gilt-framed mirror that had once belonged to Marie Antoinette.

Regular sessions with a highly skilled and discreet plastic surgeon kept her looking years younger than her true age. All the same, there was a limit to what even the most dedicated physician could achieve. Not even her considerable power could stop the remorseless onslaught of time.

She had—what?—thirty years left at the outside. No matter how hard she fought, they would ultimately be years of decline. Before that happened, before it became obvious to others, she had to put her mark on the future.

In twenty-four hours, it would all be over. After waiting so long, she could manage that much more. And then... She permitted herself a faint smile. Then she would have everything exactly as she wanted. As it was meant to be.

The supermarket was more crowded than usual, proof that Mark wasn't the only person who sensed bad weather coming. Lisa loaded her cart with all it would carry, then waited in line to pay. She was wheeling the cart out into the parking lot when a Jeep rounded the nearby corner.

The glimpse she caught of it was so fleeting that she couldn't be sure how much of what she thought she saw was real and how much imagined. All the same, a shock of fear went through her. The car looked nothing at all like the one that had followed her but, unless she was genuinely seeing things, the two men in the front seat were the same ones Mark had tangled with.

Her stomach clenched. She shoved the cart up against the truck and yanked open the rear hatch. As quickly as she could, she loaded the groceries in, then went around and jumped behind the wheel.

In the back of her mind, she'd been hoping to follow the Jeep, but by the time she turned the key in the ignition it was well out of sight. For several moments she sat with the motor running as she tried to decide what to do.

The safest course, and the one Mark would undoubtedly expect her to take, was to head straight back to the farm. She could call Nagel from there and ask if he or his men had seen anything similar.

But the thought of driving all the way back and taking the risk that the sheriff might be away from his phone stopped her. If she went over to the office instead, she'd have a better chance of at least finding someone who might be able to put her fear to rest. Or perhaps confirm that it was valid.

As it happened, Nagel was in his office. He had just finished a briefing for his staff on the steps that would be taken if the weather turned as bad as some were beginning to fear. His lean face looked thoughtful, but he shook off his preoccupation when he saw her.

"Miss Morley, what can I do for you?"

She smiled, refused his offer of coffee and sat in the chair he indicated. "I won't keep you. I've got a truckful of groceries and I'm sure you're more than busy. I just wanted to ask if you'd seen any more of those two men who were following me."

"Sure you won't have coffee? I've got tea if you prefer."

"No, thank you. About the men..."

Nagel sighed. He settled back down in his own chair, but he looked far from relaxed. Lisa got the impression of a man who had at least one too many problems to deal with.

"I was going to give Mark a call."

Her face stiffened. Softly, in a voice that was rigidly controlled, she replied, "Then it's a good thing I dropped by. You can just tell me."

As hints went, her suggestion had all the subtlety of a ten-ton rock. Still, Nagel was in no rush to comply. Instead he said, "Why don't I just call him now? You can get on the extension and we can hash this out."

"Mark's got his own problems to deal with. You've seen those men again, haven't you?"

Nagel sighed. He took a swallow of his coffee and grimaced at the bitterness. "A couple of my deputies thought they got a look at them, but they weren't sure. If it is them, they've changed cars."

"They're driving a Jeep now."

The forelegs of the sheriff's chair hit the floor with a thud. He shot her a hard, narrowed stare. "How do you know that?"

She swallowed against the constriction in her throat. Without wanting to admit it to herself, she'd come hoping Nagel would tell her what she'd thought she'd seen had been strictly in her imagination. She'd wanted soothing words, maybe an avuncular smile or two, above all assurances that her fear was exaggerated. Instead she got this.

"I saw them from the parking lot at the supermarket. It was only a glimpse so I wasn't sure, but now I am."

Nagel shook his head. "Hold on, this might just be a coincidence. There's nothing to say there can't be a couple of guys who look a little like those two and who happen to show up here."

"Not a little alike, exactly."

"You said you only got a glimpse."

"It was enough. Do you honestly think I could forget what they look like?"

"No," he admitted, "but I think you could make a mistake. People do that when their emotions are running high."

It was on the tip of her tongue to answer sarcastically but she stopped herself. Nagel didn't deserve her anger. He was just trying to be reasonable. He might even be right.

She took a deep breath, fighting for calm. Quietly she said, "I understand what you're saying, I really do. But you must understand, I can't take any chance that something will happen to Jimmy."

Nagel's hard-eyed stare faded. He looked at her sympathetically. "You've already done the smartest thing you could to keep him safe. Whoever those guys are, they probably expected you to be alone and unprotected. They were wrong on both counts."

"That doesn't seem to have discouraged them."

"We don't know for sure yet whether it has or not. But there is one thing you *can* be sure of. If it's true they've come back, they're not going to be able to hide. We'll be on top of them every second. They won't be able to turn around without bumping into one of my men. If they do anything—and I mean *anything*—that's even faintly illegal, we'll have them locked up quicker than they know what hit them."

"I appreciate that, but it won't solve the problem. Whoever those men are, they're replaceable. If you arrest them, if you even manage to run them out of town, others can be sent."

Nagel rested his elbows on the desk. In his lean, weathered face, his eyes gleamed with a hunter's instinct.

"In that case," he said, "I suggest you make sure whoever is behind this gets the message that it won't be tolerated."

Lisa stood up. She had taken enough of his time and she was anxious to get back to the house. As he walked her to the door, she said, "I've tried, believe me. I'm just afraid that I haven't gotten through."

Nagel stood aside to let her precede him. Together they emerged into the anteroom. Four deputies were on duty, unusual for a single shift but understandable if there were going to be weather problems.

Lisa cast a quick glance out the window. In the short time she'd been with the sheriff the clouds had thickened further.

"Maybe you want to try again," Nagel said as he opened the outer door for her. "Case like this, just knowing there's real opposition can be enough for a person to decide it isn't worthwhile to cause more trouble."

"Maybe," Lisa said, but with little conviction. She'd tried that when she'd threatened the anonymous caller and again when she'd attempted to make contact through her former mother-in-law. So far as she could see, both efforts had produced no results.

Yet Nagel was right, she couldn't go on like this forever. If nothing else, the fear would destroy her. Unbidden, she remembered what she'd thought when she first realized how attracted she was to Mark. She wanted to be fully alive again and besides, she was through running. One way or another, Chas was a closed book. She was going to see to it that he stayed that way.

"I'll be in touch," she said as she climbed into the truck.

Nagel nodded but his eyes were watchful. He put a hand on the door to prevent her from leaving. Softly he said, "Don't do anything rash, Lisa."

She lifted her chin and met his gaze directly. "He's my child. I'll do whatever I have to."

Before he could say anything further, she gunned the motor. Nagel stepped back quickly. She caught a glimpse of him in the rearview mirror, staring after her worriedly, but he vanished from sight as she turned a corner.

She was still thinking about the men in the Jeep and what their return might mean—if indeed they had returned—when she happened to glance out the window to her left. The shock of what she saw had the effect of a body blow. She cried out and instinctively slammed her foot down on the accelerator. The truck shot forward, almost rear-ending the vehicle in front of her.

With difficulty, she regained control but her heart was racing and her breath came in painful gasps. There was too much traffic to allow her to stop—people were coming into town from all over to get their shopping done. But she was able to turn at the next corner and head back in the direction she'd come.

By the time she got to the same stretch of road again, the man she thought she'd seen was gone—if indeed he'd ever been there. Desperately she told herself her imagination was playing a particularly nasty trick on her, but deep inside she knew better.

The men in the Jeep were forgotten. They no longer mattered. Nothing did except the horrible simplicity of what she'd just seen—a man standing quietly on a street in a town he'd never been in before, looking around with cautious interest. A tall, well-built man with hair the same sandy shade as Jimmy's and features that—even in their mature form—were as familiar to her as those she saw over a cereal bowl every morning.

Chas.

Chapter 25

"Okay," Nagel said, "I've got it. If he's in town, we'll find him. In the meantime, you stay put. Understand?"

Lisa nodded. She was in the kitchen, having just gotten back to the farm. The groceries were still in the truck. She had called the sheriff before doing anything else.

"It's going to be the same thing again, isn't it? He hasn't actually committed a crime."

"We'll take care of it," Nagel insisted. "Is Mark there?"

"No, he's still out with some of the men."

"Where's Jimmy?"

"With Sam by the barn. I'm going to bring him in as soon as I hang up."

"Go do it now. If I turn up anything, I'll call. Heard a weather report lately?"

"No, how bad is it going to be?"

"Bad. By dark, nobody in their right mind is going to be moving around outside. It just may be we end up having to rescue those New York boys, maybe your ex, too."

"Not Chas. He's had a lot of experience mountain climbing."

"A regular outdoors man?" Nagel's voice dripped sarcasm. "I'll put him up against one of our blizzards any day. For once, the weather's working in our favor. Anyone tries anything, we're going to be digging *them* out."

Lisa managed a faint smile. The sheriff sounded as though he were looking forward to seeing a handful of city slickers pitted against some old-fashioned Midwestern weather. He seemed to relish the thought.

"I still think I should wait until Mark gets back and then come into town again. If I can find Chas, have it out with him..."

"No way," Nagel said flatly. "It's a bad idea to start with, but the weather makes it impossible. You stay put. Try anything else and Fletcher will have my head, not to mention yours."

Lisa sighed. She didn't have to like what the sheriff said to admit that he was right. Whatever she could have said to Chas to try to dissuade him, it would have to wait. One look at the leaden sky was enough to convince her of that.

The clouds that had looked ominous enough at daybreak now seemed to hang so near to the earth that a man standing on a tall ladder ought to be able to scrape his fingertips against them. Their undersides were brushed with a dark gray, rendering what light managed to filter through a decidedly leaden hue.

A steady wind blew out of the north, carrying the hard edge of tundra and ice floes. Beneath it the first valiant flowers of spring drew in their leaves and seemed to crouch closer to the earth.

Once when she was a small child, Lisa remembered a snowstorm that had begun on an early spring day and had continued through the night and the next day until the world had been transformed into billowing visions of drifting white, blotting out all color, all hard edges, all angles and corners. To her child's mind, it had been a thing of wonder, but then she had viewed it from the safety of the big front windows, with the furnace humming away in the basement and a pot of her mother's best stew bubbling on the stove.

This storm, she knew, would be different.

"I have to go," she said. The groceries were still in the truck. There was a great deal to do.

"Tell Mark to call me," Nagel instructed just before he hung up.

"Where should I put this, Mommy?" Jimmy asked. He held up a box of breakfast cereal, the last of the items to be taken from the last of the many bags she had unloaded with Sam's help. Mark still wasn't back, but he was expected soon. Already, some of the ewes were safe in the barn with their lambs. The rest would be rounded up shortly.

Or so Sam assured her before he carried the supplies for the men back to the bunkhouse. He paused at the kitchen door, lifted his head to sniff the air, and said, "Just in time, too, if my nose's any judge."

"Is it going to snow?" Jimmy asked when he returned from the pantry. He hopped up on a stool beside the counter and watched her as she peeled potatoes. Until Mark returned, she thought it best to keep busy. Besides, he was sure to be hungry.

"It looks that way, honey." She'd make her mother's stew. It was hearty, everyone liked it and it tasted even better the next day. While she was at it, she might as well whip up an apple pie. Now where had she put the flour...

"What are you doing?" her son asked.

She looked up, startled. "Cooking."

"Are we having a party?"

Lisa frowned, momentarily puzzled until she glanced at the big black kettle on top of the stove and realized what the problem was. Jimmy had seen her open cans, stick food in the microwave and even whip up the occasional hamburger. He'd helped her do all that, plus put together a salad and on special mornings, fry eggs. But he'd never really seen her *cook*.

"People eat more when it snows," she explained with a smile. "I'm not sure exactly why, but they do."

Jimmy looked doubtful. He knew about snow. It fell softly against the windows and piled up on the fire escape. When he put a ruler in it, with his mommy's help, it covered up the numbers as high as the four or maybe even the six.

When it stopped, he could go out and make snowballs in the park. It was fun to roll in. He knew how to make snow angels and he had gone sledding. In a few days, it would disappear and everything would be back to normal.

"Snow is a little different here," Lisa said. She started peeling potatoes again.

He rested an arm on the counter, cupped his elbow in the palm of his hand and regarded her solemnly. "How come?"

"There's more of it."

"A lot more?"

She glanced through the panes of glass that were already beginning to frost around the edges. Softly she said, "Oh, yes, a lot more."

Mark ran a hand over his horse's neck, patting him gently. It was late afternoon but the light outside the stable made it look like evening. He was bone tired, but underneath the weariness was the knowledge of a job successfully completed.

The last of the ewes and lambs had been brought into the barn a few minutes before. Not a single animal would be lost. He could sleep that night without thinking about them out there in what promised to be one hell of a blizzard.

The horse trembled lightly under his touch. He murmured to him soothingly. "Good job, boy." Leaving an extra ration of oats in the trough and checking one last time to make sure the straw was well piled up against the outer wall, he headed for the house.

Jimmy heard him coming and ran to greet him. Mark scooped him up and tired as he was, carried the laughing boy on his shoulder into the kitchen.

Lisa's smile was strained. Once Jimmy was lowered to the floor, she ruffled her son's hair and said gently, "Go wash your hands."

Mark went over to the sink to do the same. He glanced over his shoulder at Lisa. She was obviously very anxious.

"What's wrong?" he asked.

"The two men are back. They've switched to a Jeep, and Nagel says his deputies will keep them under surveillance, at least as soon as they find them."

Mark nodded. His brows knit together. The news wasn't what he would have liked to hear, but it didn't fully account for the tension he felt in her. He reached for a towel. "What else?"

"I'm not sure..."

His gaze fastened on her white, strained face. Her eyes looked darker than he'd ever seen them. Although they were standing only a few yards apart, the distance felt much greater. She seemed to be retreating from him behind a wall he wasn't sure he could penetrate.

"Chas," she said faintly. "I thought I saw him, but by the time I got back to the same spot, there was nothing."

He wadded the towel up between his hands, squeezing it harshly. "How good a look did you get?"

"Not very," she admitted. "It was only a glimpse. But it did look very much like him."

"Did you tell Nagel?"

"I called as soon as I got here. He said they'll look for him, too, but realistically I can't expect much, especially not if they've got a bad storm to deal with."

"Did Nagel say that?"

"Not in so many words. He's trying to be reassuring. But he did suggest that I make another effort to reach Chas."

"Sounds like you may not have to," Mark said grimly. He'd figured the guy wrong. Chas had struck him as the kind of man who sent others to do his dirty work, not someone who would show up himself. Now it seemed he'd been wrong.

How much would that miscalculation cost? Even though she was trying to hide it, Lisa was obviously scared. Until the storm was over and the damage cleared, Nagel would have few resources to concentrate on the search for Chas and the others.

That was the down side. On a more positive note, the storm might turn out to be their biggest advantage. At the very least, it bought them some time.

He put the towel down and went over to the stove. The stew simmered gently. "Smells good."

She nodded and a little of the strain eased from her face. She even managed a slight smile. Outside the first billowing snowflakes began to drift past the kitchen windows.

Chapter 26

They had cleaned up after dinner and Lisa was putting Jimmy to bed when Nagel called. Mark answered the phone. As soon as he heard who was on the other end, he lowered his voice.

The sheriff wouldn't be calling at that hour unless he had news. Whatever it was, Lisa would have to know, but he wanted to be able to tell her in his own way.

"Glad I got you," Nagel said, his way of acknowledging what they both understood, that the business of protection couldn't be left to one woman, no matter how courageous and determined she was.

"What's up?"

"Our boy walked up to one of my deputies on Main Street a few minutes ago and asked him if he had any idea where Lisa Morley could be found."

"He did *what?*"

"You heard me. Seems he'd been to the house and tipped to the fact that she isn't staying there."

"So he asked a deputy?" Mark was incredulous. This made absolutely no sense. If the man was really after Jimmy—or Jimmy and Lisa—he'd hardly go out of his way to notify the law of his interest.

Unless, that was, he hadn't spent enough time with the good Dr. Walters and was still crazy as a fruitcake.

"What'd the deputy do?" Mark asked.

"Told him he didn't have that information and suggested he come by the station house where he was assured we'd be completely cooperative."

"Nice try."

"Yeah," Nagel said apologetically. "All things considered, it wasn't bad. There were no grounds to detain him, he wasn't acting suspiciously, nothing. I've got to give the deputy credit, he did the best he could."

"But it didn't work?"

"No, and we aren't sure why. My deputy thinks Howell picked up on something, realized the invitation to the station house wasn't as innocent as it sounded. He said thanks but no thanks and took off."

"Did the deputy follow?"

"He tried, but Howell was on foot and apparently he moves fast. He realized he was being followed and disappeared down an alley. He hasn't been seen since."

Mark glanced at the clock on the kitchen wall. It was almost seven. The storm had brought early darkness. An inch of snow had already accumulated on the windowsill. He was sure it was only the first of many.

"All the stores are closed by now, right?" he asked.

"You bet. Everybody wanted to get home ahead of the weather."

"So there aren't going to be a whole lot of people around for Howell to ask about Lisa. He's on his own."

"Pretty much, unless you count the two other guys."

"I don't get that," Mark said slowly. "They've been in town long enough to know where Lisa is staying, so how come they haven't told him?"

"Beats me. Maybe they haven't had an opportunity. Anyway, Howell's going to have to get inside soon or get out of the area altogether. I figure you should be okay for tonight and well into tomorrow. The forecast is for a foot and a half by morning. It'll be a good twenty-four hours before the roads are cleared."

"There's no rush as far as I'm concerned," Mark said.

"How's Lisa holding up?"

"About as well as you'd expect."

"She tell you about coming to see me?"

"Yeah, she did. You think she's right about the other two being back?"

"Stands to reason if Howell is here, his people would be, too."

"I suppose," Mark agreed.

"Listen, I've got a lot of respect for Lisa and I don't blame her for wanting to keep her boy safe at all costs. But I'm a little worried she might do something she shouldn't."

"I'll keep an eye on her."

"I know you will. Just remember, whatever Howell's up to, if he breaks the law, he's mine."

"That's coming into the game a little late, don't you think?"

Nagel's voice hardened. "I mean it, Mark. This isn't a hockey rink. Let us handle it."

"That's fine with me."

The sheriff was silent for a moment. Mark's easy compliance clearly surprised him. He didn't trust it and he was smart not to.

Nagel was a good man, devoted to his job. But he was hamstrung by a law that let a woman be stalked like an animal and was powerless to help her until she was actually injured or worse.

"Snow's coming faster," he said.

"I better be going. Remember what I said?"

Mark assured him that he would and hung up. For several minutes he sat, listening to the soft sounds coming from the bedroom down the hall.

Lisa was reading Jimmy a story. He imagined her with the sleepy child cuddled in the crook of her arm, murmuring gently as she wove spells of love and security.

That this child was not of his own making didn't even occur to Mark. He already liked Jimmy fine. With no effort at all, he would love him. He was a great kid, thanks to Lisa. She was a fantastic woman, warm, strong, nurturing. It wasn't hard to imagine her with more kids, hazel-eyed like her and Jimmy, filling the house with life and laughter.

Not hard at all.

A grim smile curved his mouth. Chas was fast, was he? He couldn't be fast enough to elude Mark.

It had been a lot of years since he'd gone hunting and when he had, it hadn't been for sport. He'd killed for food, for survival. That had a way of concentrating a man's attention and honing his skills until they were purely lethal.

All the same, he'd never really enjoyed the hunt. It had just been something he had to do. This time would be different. This time he'd like it just fine.

Lisa came back to the kitchen a few minutes later. Mark was still sitting at the kitchen table. He had a snowshoe propped between his legs and was checking the webbing on it.

"Jimmy's asleep already. I guess the last few days have tired him out."

"Looks like they've done the same to you."

She sighed and brushed a stray lock of hair from her forehead. "It's the not knowing that I hate. I just want this over with so I can get on with my life."

He nodded silently even as he resisted the impulse to ask her how she saw that life. What did she hope for and dream of when she thought of the future. She'd said that she came back to Langston to stay, but he still wasn't absolutely sure that she meant it. Fear might keep her moving on—unless he could put an end to it, once and for all.

"You should get some rest," he said quietly.

"You, too."

"I'm going to sit up for a while."

She glanced at the snowshoe. "What's that for?"

"Just a precaution. We still don't know how bad it's going to be."

Lisa nodded absently. She looked as though she were out on her feet.

Mark put the snowshoe aside and stood up. Gently he took hold of her shoulders and pointed her in the direction of the door. "Don't you remember how good it feels to sleep on nights when there's a blizzard?"

"As a matter of fact, I do." She shot him a grateful look and touched her lips to his lightly. "Thank you."

"For what?"

"Everything." Her perfume lingered on the air long after she'd gone.

Lisa took a long shower, letting the hot water wash away the stress that had been building in her since morning. Mark was right. She felt as though she barely had the strength to stand. Fear and tension had taken their usual toll.

Finally she got out and wrapped in her robe, went down the hall to check on Jimmy. He was deeply asleep, clutching his bear.

Satisfied, she returned to her room and slipped into a nightgown. The golden silk slithered over her body, falling to her feet. The thin straps and low-cut bodice left a good deal of gleaming skin bare but she still felt comfortable. Despite the snow that was now falling steadily, the house was warm.

Paradoxically, she no longer felt as tired. The thought of bed—especially a solitary one—had little appeal. On impulse, she left the room.

The kitchen was empty. Mark had left the snowshoes by the back door. She felt a spurt of disappointment at the thought that he had already turned in. About to do the same herself, she caught a whiff of wood smoke from the great room.

He was there, sitting in front of the fire, dressed only in pajama bottoms. The broad expanse of his chest looked burnished by the flames. He appeared deep in thought yet he was instantly aware of her presence.

Mark held out a hand to her. She came in answer to this silent summons and settled beside him on the couch. Neither spoke. It was enough to be there, together, as snow beat against the high windows and night wrapped itself around the house.

At some point Lisa drifted off to sleep. She woke an unknown time later. The fire had died down and outside the snow was coming faster than ever. Otherwise everything seemed the same except that Mark, too, was awake.

"Did you hear something?" he asked.

"I don't know. I was alseep."

"So was I." He stood up, glancing around. "I could have sworn..."

Abruptly he was moving in the direction of the bedrooms. Lisa followed. Her throat was suddenly tight and a wild clamor had begun deep down in her mind. She told herself not to panic, everything was fine. It was only natural that they should both be worried, but there was no reason for fear... no reason at all.

The window of Jimmy's room was open. Wind thrust the curtains inside and snow littered the floor.

Except for a battered bear, the bed was empty.

Chapter 27

"You aren't going," Mark said. He spoke through clenched teeth. It was scant moments since they had discovered Jimmy's disappearance. The shock still burned in him but within seconds he was in motion.

He yanked clothes from the closet and dragged them on, all the while thinking fast. A quick glance out the window had been enough to confirm that Jimmy had not just been taken. What footprints could be seen were already well filled in with fresh snow.

The sound that had awakened them was the crack of a branch outside the window. Had the window been properly closed, they wouldn't have heard it. On some subconscious level their minds must have realized that, for otherwise they would hardly have noticed.

Judging by the rate of snowfall and the condition of the footprints, he'd been taken at least half an hour before. Mark's face was grim as he finished dressing.

Every moment was precious. He had no time to argue with Lisa.

"The hell I'm not," she said. She, too, was dressing, having brought the clothes in from her room. Her face was ashen and her hands shook but she looked fiercely determined.

"Be sensible. This blizzard's barely started. By morning, it's going to be impassable out there. You won't be able to keep up."

"Watch me," she said as she pulled up the zipper on her jeans and jammed her feet into boots.

Mark cursed under his breath. He could try to convince her but he already knew it would be useless. Nor could he really blame her. Maybe some women could have waited in relative comfort and safety for news of their child, but Lisa wasn't one of them. Like it or not, she was coming.

"Call Nagel," he instructed. "Tell him to get the deputies out and notify the state troopers. I'll get Sam and the others."

She nodded and ran to do as he bid. Within minutes, they were ready. Mark rode the big gray while Lisa chose a smaller mount, a mare whose seeming delicacy hid a fierce spirit. The men also rode out— Sam and five others—taking all the available horses.

In front of the barn, they paused as the horses pawed the snow-covered ground and tossed their heads at the swirling flakes. With each passing moment, the blizzard worsened. Lisa stared into it and shuddered.

If she let herself think about Jimmy, let herself imagine what he was enduring, she would start to scream and she had no assurance that she'd be able to stop. Instead she thought of Chas and what she would do when they met.

Sam and the other men split up into teams of two and headed out in different directions. Mark turned the stallion's head toward the way he had reserved for them, north.

Lisa hadn't ridden in a long time. For the first few minutes she was fully occupied becoming accustomed to the mare. They were some distance from the house before she thought to ask, "Why this way?"

"We're going toward the closest road. I figure he had to have a vehicle parked nearby. There'll be almost no traffic tonight. We may be able to pick up tracks."

It seemed little enough to go on, but she couldn't suggest an alternative. A gust of snow blew in her face, momentarily blinding her. The mare tossed her head and continued on, following in the wake of the stallion.

Lisa quickly lost track of time. She had no idea how far they were from the house, only that it had long since vanished into the swirling white mass behind them. There was no way to go except forward.

Mark had brought a powerful light that he shone in front of them. It picked up the white glare of what was now a full-fledged blizzard, one of the worst she'd ever seen. Again she thought of Jimmy and had to suppress the roiling black terror that rose within her.

At last, Mark drew rein and she was able to come up beside him. Over the rush of the wind, she asked, "How much farther?"

"Not long," he replied, raising an arm and pointing ahead. "Look."

She stared in the direction he indicated. At first nothing appeared to have changed. It was only after she'd gazed straight ahead for several moments that she realized the ground ahead was flatter and more regularly shaped than what they had passed over.

Slowly, her lips stiff with cold, she said, "The road."

Mark nodded. He pulled his wide-brimmed hat down on his head more securely and, reaching out, did the same to hers.

They were both bundled in sheepskin coats, both boot-shod and gloved. But the cold was becoming intense. Any exposed skin risked frostbite.

"Pull that scarf up over your nose," he directed.

She did as he said. They moved on, reaching the road a short time later. There they paused. Mark rose in his saddle, turning the light in either direction.

"Which way?" Lisa called above the wind. It was becoming so fierce that she almost had to shout to be heard. Her skin above the scarf was no longer cold. Instead, it seemed to burn.

She ducked her head farther down into the wide collar of her coat and slipped a hand beneath the sheepskin. Her fingers brushed icy metal.

She withdrew her hand but the hilt of the gun continued to press into her, an inexorable reminder of her desperation and exactly how far it might drive her.

"That way," Mark said, pointing to the right. "Toward town."

"I don't see any tracks."

"Wait," he advised. "Good old Chas may be a nut case, but I'm not convinced he's stupid. He'd realize he couldn't get far in this weather and he'd need to hole up. Town would be his best bet."

"He'll never make it," Lisa cried above the wind. "The drifts are already too high."

Mark nodded grimly. Although the blizzard was only a few hours old and had far longer to go, the wind had already whipped sizable drifts up along the road. Even a four-wheel-drive vehicle would have trouble getting by.

"Nagel and the deputies won't get far," he said.

"They're using a plow, trying to cut through."

Mark said nothing more, but the same thought was in both their minds—with the temperature falling and the blizzard still worsening, by the time the sheriff reached them, it might be too late. Chas could vanish into the storm and Jimmy with him.

"Look," Mark shouted. He shone the light on the crystalline snow ahead of them. Lisa peered through it. She could just make out the telltale tread of tires.

"Oh, God," she whispered fervently, "let it be him."

Despite the wind, Mark heard her. He nodded, adding his own silent plea. They plunged on, following the trail, but before they could get very far, the light collided against a dark shape up ahead on the road.

"What's that?" Lisa called.

"Can't tell yet. Could be a car."

She took a deep breath and pressed her heels to the mare's sides. *"Jimmy!"*

There was no answer, nor had she expected any. Her heart was pounding as they came up to the vehicle. Just then the wind blew with especial viciousness, lifting the snow from a section of the car, enough to reveal the bright gleam of red.

"The Jeep," Mark said. He dismounted quickly and handed the gray's reins to Lisa. "Hold onto him. Don't let him buck."

Occupied with keeping the bigger horse calm, she still tried to get a glimpse in the vehicle. Something seemed to be moving inside. Her lips moved in heart-felt prayer.

Mark yanked the door open. A big, bulky shape slid forward, almost falling onto the road. Virulent curses filled the air.

"Where is he?" the man demanded. "Damn it, when I get my hands on that SOB, he'll—"

"Shut up," Mark interrupted. He shoved the man back into the Jeep but not before taking a quick, thorough look inside. A second man leaned forward, his face ashen with fear, his hands also tied behind his back, as were the first man's.

"What the hell do you think you're doing? You can't leave us here like this."

"The sheriff's coming with a plow," Mark said. He spoke matter-of-factly, as though an expectation had been fulfilled. "He'll get you out. In the meantime, you tell me, which way did Howell go?"

"To hell," the man said, glaring at Mark. "Why don't you follow him?"

"Why don't I just push your Jeep off the road so the sheriff goes right by without spotting it?"

"You wouldn't . . ."

"In a second. Now where's Howell?"

"I don't know," the man said. "I swear."

"It's true," the second chimed in. "He took us by surprise. We didn't even know he was there. One second we had the kid, the next minute we were both trussed up like a couple of chickens."

"*You* had him?" Lisa exclaimed. "What are you talking about?"

"Later," Mark said firmly. He took the reins from her and remounted quickly. "There's no time now. Howell's better than I thought, not to mention smarter. We've got to find him before he gets too far."

From the saddle, he looked down at the two men huddled in the Jeep. "What's he driving?"

"Sno-Cat."

Mark cursed. He kicked the door shut and turned to Lisa. "This is bad. Unlike these two bozos, he came prepared. He can outpace us and he doesn't have to stay on the road."

"We have to find him. We *have* to."

"I know," he said quietly. The lines of his face were more harshly drawn than she had ever seen them. He lifted his head into the storm, his big, hard body drawn taut, all his senses painfully alert.

After a moment he said, "This way."

Half a mile out of town, the road dipped between rocky outcroppings that stood a good fifty feet high. There the snow had settled between delicately poised crevasses, slipping between adjoining surfaces, working its wet, slick way down through pebbles and boulders alike.

It might not have made any difference. A hundred snowfalls could have come and gone without effect. But on that night, in that place, the snow had fallen in just such a way as to unbalance one small stone and then another and another until they'd surged against the larger rocks, tipping them just enough to let gravity do the rest.

The rock slide hadn't been large, just big enough to block the road and put a few dents in the Sno-Cat Mark and Lisa found abandoned there.

Chapter 28

"One set of footprints," Mark reported. "Man-size. How tall is good old Chas?"

"About your height," Lisa replied. Her voice was choked. She could no longer avoid thoughts about Jimmy. He was in terrible and immediate danger, yet she was powerless to help him. It was more than she could possibly bear.

"Your height," she repeated dully. The light had gone out of her eyes. As hope receded, something else entirely took its place, the simple human need to return the pain being inflicted on her.

To seek revenge.

"His stride is short," Mark murmured, almost to himself. "Looks as though he's carrying something."

"Jimmy?"

"Has to be," he said as he remounted. "Also, unless I miss my guess, he did at least a quick surveillance of the area before the storm hit."

"Why do you say that?" She really wasn't interested, but *not* to ask might arouse Mark's suspicions. It might give him some clue as to the direction of her thoughts.

"Because there's a herder's shed in that direction. It's the only shelter anywhere around here."

A tiny flicker of excitement sparked within her. But the relentless wind and cold kept it from growing. All the same, she followed Mark. There was nothing else to do.

The shed was a quarter mile away from the road, not much on a nice spring day but an infinity on such a night. Even on horseback, they had trouble negotiating the distance.

Mark insisted on going slowly and she didn't have to ask why. Every rounded mound of snow had to be checked at least visually lest it conceal a fallen man and the small boy they both prayed he still had with him.

If Jimmy had managed to get away from his father... if he had run into the storm alone...

Lisa bit down hard enough on her lower lip to draw blood. Tears were frozen to her cheeks. Every passing moment brought new anguish.

"How much longer?" she asked above the wind.

Mark raised an arm, pointing. "There."

Just ahead she could make out a low, indistinct blur half covered by snow. The shed. Determination gripped her. Again she slipped her hand inside the jacket, feeling for the gun.

"I'll go first," Mark said. They dismounted together, securing the horses to the top of a post that still emerged from the drifting snow. A faint light shone inside. The door was little more than a few planks nailed together.

A loud crack sounded above the wind as Mark shoved the door in. He followed hard and fast, hoping to give no one inside time to react. But the man he confronted was already on his feet, standing directly in front of a small, huddled shape on the floor.

The man didn't hesitate. Before Mark was barely inside, he launched himself at him.

Lisa reached the door. In an instant, she took in the two big, hard men struggling with all their strength. They were well matched. Mark slightly larger and more muscular, but both in peak condition and both fiercely determined.

Her glance shifted. She saw the shape on the floor and took a quick, urgent step toward it. At the same moment Chas landed a brutal blow to Mark's midsection, hurtling him against the wall. That should have been enough to incapacitate most men, but he was only momentarily winded. Struggling to his feet, teeth bared, he came at his opponent again. But not before Chas took advantage of the tiny edge he'd just gained. Cold metal gleamed in the shadowed light. The blade he pulled from his boot was darkly lethal, curved toward the tip, meant for killing.

Mark, not seeing the weapon, moved straight toward it.

Lisa's hand closed on the gun. She pulled it out from beneath the jacket. Her heart was pounding. Bile burned the back of her throat. For the merest second, she hesitated.

"Mommy, no!"

The small, huddled shape resolved itself into Jimmy. Pale, disheveled, and wrapped in what was appar-

ently Chas's jacket for Chas was wearing none. Bless-
edly alive and seemingly unharmed.

"Don't," he screamed, and threw himself at her.

Instinctively she dropped the gun. It had barely hit
the floor of the shed before he was caught in her arms,
solid and real against her, a small, sobbing presence
babbling about bad men and his father, the storm, and
about Chas carrying him and telling him everything
would be all right.

"He said he'd get me back to you, Mommy. He said
not to be scared."

Chas froze. He stared from the woman and child to
the man before him, pale now and deeply shaken, the
knife falling from his hand as he closed his eyes in un-
feigned relief.

"Thank God," Chas said, then he slipped uncon-
scious to the floor.

"All things considered, he's in pretty good shape,"
Nagel said. They were standing in the hallway outside
Chas's room in the small hospital that served Lang-
ston.

The trip there was little more than a blur to Lisa.
She remembered Mark hoisting Chas up onto his
horse as she held Jimmy in front of her on the mare.
Mercifully, they had reached town without further in-
cident.

The hospital was fully staffed in expectation of ca-
sualties from the storm. Chas was rushed right into
emergency. A doctor came out some time later to report that while he was suffering from exposure and a
couple of nasty blows—this with a particular look at
Mark—he would recover completely.

Nagel had already sent deputies to bring in the two men from the Jeep. They, too, would receive any necessary medical care, but they would be spending the night in jail. The first of many they would spend that way, considering what Lisa had already learned from Jimmy.

"I'd like to see him," she said quietly.

The sheriff shrugged. "Up to you, but tell me first, am I supposed to charge him with something or not?"

She paused at the door. Over her shoulder, she said, "Only if it's a crime to have the wrong mother."

Chas was sitting up in bed. His head was bandaged and he looked pale. A very pretty nurse was keeping him company. She glanced up as Lisa entered.

"Mr. Howell isn't up to visitors yet...."

"It's all right," Chas said. He shot her a devilish smile that made her cheeks warm. "In such good hands I have to be feeling better."

Lisa shook her head ruefully. She waited until the nurse left, a little dazedly, before she said, "Still the same, I see. Getting by on charm."

"And good looks," he added. "Don't forget those."

"Actually, you're looking a little worse for the wear at the moment."

Chas grimaced. He put a hand to his jaw, where a purple-bluish bruise was already darkening. "Thanks to that friend of yours." He tried to smile again but couldn't quite manage it, not surprisingly, considering the fact he'd plowed through a blizzard—carrying a small boy wrapped in his jacket—risking frostbite and worse to get Jimmy away from the men who had kidnapped him.

"Why?" Lisa asked. She sat down on the edge of the bed and studied Chas calmly. He looked little different from what she remembered, yet he seemed completely changed. Certainly she no longer saw him in the same light.

The last time she had seen him he'd been walking out of her life, abandoning her and the child she was carrying in all ways except the strictly financial. She had been stunned, disbelieving, afraid and more than a little angry.

Now he was back, and she wanted answers. The ones she should have gotten four years before plus a few more.

"Those men were working for your mother, weren't they?"

Chas nodded. "How did you know?"

"Jimmy told me. He said they told him they were taking him to his grandmother and that he heard them talking about how much she was paying."

Pain flitted across Chas's face. It wasn't strictly physical. "This is very hard," he said.

Lisa reached out across the bed and took his hand. She felt nothing, only the need to give comfort. Softly she said, "I know about Dr. Walters."

Chas's eyes widened. He drew back slightly but he didn't remove his hand. "How?"

"I found the notations in your address book. You were seeing a psychiatrist while we were married and you never told me. Why?"

His smile was filled with self-mockery. "It didn't exactly fit the picture, did it?"

"Picture?"

"Prince Charming, the guy on the white horse. The one who came riding into your life and swept you away. Remember?"

Lisa's hand tightened on his. "Is that how I seemed? A naive girl who just expected to live happily ever after?"

"No," Chas said quietly. "You seemed real, incredibly alive and filled with strength. Everything I needed most. The problem was that the longer I stayed with you, the more I became afraid that I'd end up hurting you. And when you told me about the baby..."

He looked away, staring sightlessly at the blank hospital wall. "I knew I couldn't be a father. I'd be a disaster at it. The best thing to do was just to leave."

Lisa shook her head slowly. Thoughts tumbled through her mind, half remembered comments and allusions. A pattern was beginning to form but she still couldn't see it clearly.

"I don't understand. This has something to do with your mother, but—"

"You spoke with her."

"That's right, yesterday, but—"

"No, *before,* when she was calling you. You thought she was me and you threatened to do anything you had to to protect Jimmy. She thought that was very funny."

Lisa shook her head, not understanding. "Why would she—?"

Chas was silent for a moment, his eyes shadowed with pain. Softly he said, "She likes to have her own way. She'll go to any lengths to get it. Any lengths at all. Control is very important to her. She lives for it. There were times when she'd hold me in her arms and tell me how wonderful I was, what a good boy, exactly the son she wanted." He paused, looking away from Lisa as though he couldn't bear to face her and say the words that had to be said.

"And then there were the other times, when I'd do something she didn't like, anything at all, and she'd get angry. She had to be in control. The moment that was threatened, she snapped. I . . . endured the beatings until I was nine. I grew fast, and by then I was big enough to get away from her, but the damage was already done."

He took a deep breath. Quietly he said it again. "I was terrified when you told me you were pregnant. On the one hand, I certainly hadn't done anything to prevent it or even told you that I didn't want to have children. Somewhere deep inside I *did* want it—desperately. But I was also afraid that I'd been damaged enough—twisted enough—that I would end up doing to a child what my mother had done to me."

"No!" Lisa cried out. Her throat was very tight and tears burned her eyes. Instinctively she reached for him, but he covered her hands with his own and squeezed gently.

"Yes," he said. "It happens that way. One generation passes it on to the next. I think my mother was consciously trying to make me like her. For a long time, I didn't know if she'd succeeded or not."

"She didn't," Lisa insisted. "You never hurt Jimmy. You saved him."

"Yes," Chas said, almost on a note of wonder. "I did. He's so beautiful, so incredibly real. All I could think of while I was with him was what a fantastic job you've done."

He looked up, meeting her eyes. "Mother knew she'd failed with me even before I realized it. That's why she wanted Jimmy. He was her chance to start over, to control the next generation. That's all that matters to her. She was willing to go to any lengths to get him."

"And you found out?" Lisa asked. Pity welled up in her, but she did her best to conceal it. For all he had suffered, Chas was a proud man.

He nodded. "She made the mistake of contacting me. We hadn't spoken in years, but that didn't stop her from making demands. I was supposed to bring Jimmy to her. When I refused and told her she was crazy, she said she'd get what she wanted another way, and hung up. That's when I started looking for you."

"But I'd already left New York?"

"That's right. There were men watching your building, trying to find out where you'd gone. As near as I can figure, they bribed somebody at the post office to read off the address where your friend, the superintendent, was mailing you stuff. Once they had that, they were on their way."

"With you tailing them? Why didn't you just warn me?"

"Because I couldn't find you. You weren't at your parents' house and when I tried to find out where you'd gone, I got the feeling the question wasn't exactly welcome."

"The deputy invited you back to the station house," Lisa said with a faint smile.

Chas nodded. "For what promised to be a real long chat. I didn't have time for that, not with those two goons ready to move in. Fortunately I spotted them heading out of town and followed." He shook his head ruefully. "I couldn't believe they'd be stupid enough to try to snatch Jimmy during a blizzard. But either they hadn't listened to the weather reports or they didn't believe them. Then when the Sno-Cat got hit by the rocks, I figured there was nothing to do except get him to shelter."

"At the risk of your own life," Lisa said quietly.

Chas shifted in the bed. He was uncomfortable even with unspoken praise. "I've been a lousy father. He didn't ask for that and he sure as hell didn't ask for a grandmother who's certifiable. The least I could do was protect him."

"What happens now?" she asked.

"The men will testify against my mother." His tone of voice and the look in his eyes made it clear they wouldn't have any choice.

"Do you mean in a court of law?" Lisa asked. She was thinking about what it would mean to Jimmy to be put through such an experience.

Chas shook his head. "At a competency hearing, that's all. I meant it when I said she's certifiable. She's going to spend the remainder of her life in a place where she can't hurt anyone, including herself."

He hesitated, looking at Lisa. Quietly he said, "There's no way I can ever make up to you for what you've been through. But I can promise you it's over. I walked away four years ago because I honestly believed I was too affected inside by what had happened to me as a child to be a decent husband, let alone a father. I'm still not sure I'll ever be capable of either, but I do know that nothing to do with the Howells will ever hurt you again."

Lisa believed him. It was impossible not to. With a start, she realized that in an important sense she had never really known Chas. He'd hurt so much inside that he'd kept a great deal of himself from her.

But that was changed. The need to protect his son had at last brought him face-to-face with his own demons, and enabled him to conquer them.

"I do have one favor to ask," he said. "If you want to say no, I understand."

Lisa blinked back the tears that still threatened to fall. Later she could cry for the child he had been and the man he had at last become, but not now. "What is it?"

"I'll be checking out of here in the morning, heading back to New York. Before I go, I'd like to see Jimmy again."

"He's asleep in a room down the hall."

"I understand. You don't want to wake him...."

"He does need to rest, but he can have breakfast with you, if you like."

Chas stared at her. Slowly he nodded. "You're a generous woman."

Lisa slipped her hand from his. She thought of Mark waiting outside, giving her this time to put the past to rest. Standing, she said, "And a lucky one."

Outside in the corridor, she walked down to where Jimmy was sleeping and looked in on him. He lay on his side, holding the bear she'd brought tucked under her jacket. His lips were slightly parted and he appeared to be smiling. For several minutes, she knelt beside him, giving thanks for all that had been given to her.

When she came back into the hallway, Mark was there. Silently he opened his arms.

Without hesitation, Lisa went to him.

Epilogue

Night wrapped round like a silken blanket, soothing the raveled care of day, stilling anxious thought and bestowing peace. Outside the snow had stopped. Already a warmer wind, almost balmy by contrast, blew over the white-encrusted ground. Through the open window Lisa listened to the slow drip-drip of melted snow running away into the earth.

Mark stirred beside her. Beneath her cheek, she felt the slow, steady beat of his heart. Her hand curled on his chest, close by his warmth, as a smile curved her lips.

"It's over," she whispered, her breath brushing his burnished skin.

He turned slightly, drawing her closer, and lifted her chin so that their eyes met. "Is it?"

"Oh, yes," she said, and her smile was filled with such freedom and joy that he couldn't help but believe her. "It really is."

He smiled then, too, touched, in turn, by this woman's happiness far more than he would have had it been his own. And yet, in a sense, it was.

She'd told him everything Chas had revealed to her, weeping as she did so, unashamed of the tears for she understood them to be both right and necessary. As did he, survivor as he was of a failed parent of his own although one ultimately less threatening than *Mother* Howell. Had any woman ever been less deserving of the name?

"Chas is a good guy," he murmured. "That's amazing, all things considered." He paused, feeling his way. The words were hard, but he felt they had to be said.

"Given half a chance, he'd be a good father, too."

To his relief, Lisa nodded. She wasn't offended or threatened by that observation. On the contrary, she agreed with it.

"When we've all had some time to come to terms with what's happened, I'm going to encourage him to see Jimmy."

"That shouldn't take much persuading."

"No, I don't think it will. But, Mark—" She broke off, raising herself on her elbows so she could see him more clearly. "There's something I want you to know. You've been the first father Jimmy's ever really had. I hope you realize he's going to go on thinking of you that way."

Deeply moved, he touched a finger to the damask-smooth cheek still flushed from their lovemaking. Her eyes were bright, the shadows gone. She looked at him with complete trust and—

His breath caught. Always before, even when their passion reached heights he had never before known, he'd sensed her holding back somewhat, still burdened by the past. But not this time, not now, here in this softening night as spring once again claimed the land.

"I love you," he said. The words came without hesitation, as freely as the radiant smile she gave him.

"I love you," she murmured, and traced the beard-roughened line of his jaw with the smooth pink tip of her tongue, teasing lightly at the corner of his mouth.

He sighed, a rueful, completely male sound that made her sit up and take notice. Her eyes widened.

"Again?"

"You have this strange effect on me. I'll probably die from it, but what the heck—"

"Not if I have anything to say about it," she said, and looked directly at him.

He saw the question in her eyes and marveled that she could harbor any doubt. Quickly, he moved to still it, once and for all.

"You do," he said, "most definitely." One last small spark of hesitation, sputtering here on the brink of all he had ever dared to dream, flared briefly and then went out, unmissed. "That is, if you can stand being an over-the-hill hockey player's wife."

"I can stand being yours," she said, and moved into the loving circle of his arms.

* * * * *

AMERICAN HERO

You have spoken! You've asked for more of our irresistible American Heroes, and now we're happy to oblige. After all, we're as in love with these men as you are! In coming months, look for these must-have guys:

In COLD, COLD HEART (IM #487) by Ann Williams, we're looking at a hero with a heart of ice. But when faced with a desperate mother and a missing child, his heart begins to melt. You'll want to be there in April to see the results!

In May we celebrate the line's tenth anniversary with one of our most-requested heroes ever: Quinn Eisley. In QUINN EISLEY'S WAR (IM #493) by Patricia Gardner Evans, this lone-wolf agent finally meets the one woman who is his perfect match.

The weather starts to heat up in June, so come deep-sea diving with us in Heather Graham Pozzessere's BETWEEN ROC AND A HARD PLACE (IM #499). Your blood will boil right along with Roc Trellyn's when he pulls in his net to find—his not-quite-ex-wife!

AMERICAN HEROES. YOU WON'T WANT TO MISS A SINGLE ONE—ONLY FROM

INTIMATE MOMENTS®
Silhouette®

IMHER04

INTIMATE MOMENTS

10TH *Anniversary*

Celebrate our anniversary with a fabulous collection of firsts....

The first Intimate Moments titles written by three of your favorite authors:

NIGHT MOVES   Heather Graham Pozzessere
LADY OF THE NIGHT Emilie Richards
A STRANGER'S SMILE Kathleen Korbel

Silhouette Intimate Moments is proud to present a FREE hardbound collection of our authors' firsts—titles that you will treasure in the years to come from some of the line's founding members.

This collection will not be sold in retail stores and is available only through this exclusive offer. Look for details in Silhouette Intimate Moments titles available in retail stores in May, June and July.

Silhouette Books
is proud to present
our best authors,
their best books...
and the best in
your reading pleasure!

Throughout 1993, look for exciting books
by these top names in contemporary
romance:

CATHERINE COULTER—
Aftershocks in February

FERN MICHAELS—
Nightstar in March

DIANA PALMER—
Heather's Song in March

ELIZABETH LOWELL
Love Song for a Raven in April

SANDRA BROWN
(previously published under
the pseudonym Erin St. Claire)—
Led Astray in April

LINDA HOWARD—
All That Glitters in May

When it comes to passion,
we wrote the book.

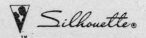

BOBT1RR